LeRoy Collins Leon Co.
Public Library System
200 West Park Avenue
Tallahassee, FL 32301

DEDICATION

This story is dedicated to the memory of the cadets of the West Florida Seminary, who when called upon to defend their homeland, went bravely forth to do their duty.

It is also dedicated to all my Civil War reenacting friends in the Leon Rifles, especially, Mark Rominger, Chris Ellrich, Buzz Gifford, Bill Pfeil, Jim Willenbrink, Don Mixon, Mike DeVaney, and last but not least "English" Mike Fawcett.

ACKNOWLEDGEMENTS

I wish to thank the Sarvis family for allowing me to use their great-great-great-grandfather, Luther Tucker, as one of my main characters in this story. Cadet Luther Tucker actually fought at the Battle of Natural Bridge. His remains are buried in a cemetery near Sopchoppy, Florida.

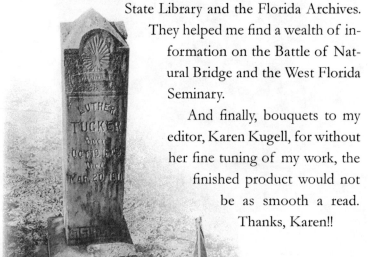

I owe a debt of thanks to the helpful staff of the Florida State Library and the Florida Archives. They helped me find a wealth of information on the Battle of Natural Bridge and the West Florida Seminary.

And finally, bouquets to my editor, Karen Kugell, for without her fine tuning of my work, the finished product would not be as smooth a read. Thanks, Karen!!

Author's Note

This is a work of fiction. It is not intended to be a history of the Battle of Natural Bridge, but rather a story of the experiences of a West Florida Seminary cadet during the last months of the Civil War. It's a blend of Florida history and my imagination. Please keep in mind that the characters in the story are purely fictional and any resemblance to real people is coincidental.

In doing my research I often found more than one version of the events surrounding the Battle of Natural Bridge. Since this is a fictional story I usually picked the more interesting version as my guide to the plot.

Many of the characters in my story have varying opinions about politics and the war. While reading this novel, please remember that they do not necessarily share my beliefs.

I hope you will have as much fun reading my story as I had writing it!

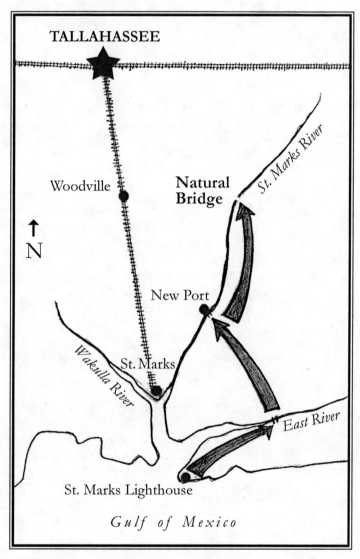

The Union advances on Tallahassee, early March 1865.

Chapter 1

It was a cold, windy morning in February 1865. I shivered as I stood in the front of two ranks waiting for Captain Johnson to begin our color ceremony. A strong gust of wind suddenly blew at us from out of the north, cutting through our cadet jackets like a knife cutting through butter. Burr!!! I couldn't stop shivering, and I wished I was back home in Monticello, under three blankets, warm and cozy.

Behind me stood the main building of the West Florida Seminary, a two story, white Greek Revival building with four massive Doric columns supporting the front portico.

As we waited for the captain, I looked down Clinton Avenue where a pale winter sun could be seen peeking over the rooftops of Tallahassee. At the highest point of the hill, just off to my right, I observed that familiar sight, our state's capitol building, the pride of this small town.

"I wish the captain would get this thing started. I'm freezing here!" whispered a voice behind me.

It was my best friend, Luther Tucker, standing in the rear rank. He was 16 years old, just like myself, and was a tall slim handsome young man, with a good head on his shoulders. He was from a good Wakulla County family, and made a great buddy. We shared bunks in the dormitory. He had the top and I had the bottom.

What was the captain waiting for, I wondered?

Captain Valentine Mason Johnson was a graduate of the Virginia Military Institute, class of '60. During 1861-1862 he served as the captain of a company in the 30th Virginia Infantry. But in 1863 his health failed, so he moved to Tallahassee where he became the assistant principal of the West Florida Seminary. When the principal resigned in February 1864, Johnson became our new principal.

The captain was dressed in a Confederate gray double-breasted frock coat with shiny brass buttons. He wore a kepi with gold braid, had a fine mustache, and at last, stepped out smartly to a position directly in front of his cadets.

"Attention, company!" he shouted.

"Color guard, post!"

A pair of cadets marched to the flagpole. They hooked up the Second National Flag, the official flag of the Confederacy since 1863.

"Present, arms!" commanded the captain.

As the flag went up the pole, each and every cadet moved his musket to the position of "present, arms", while our drummer, Dick, and our fife player, Charlie, played the National Anthem, Dixie.

"Shoulder, arms."

"Order, arms."

"In place, rest," the captain gave us the command to stand at ease.

Captain Johnson looked over the formation of cadets in front of him. We ranged in ages from ten to seventeen. At the start of the war, in 1861, we had 250 students attending the seminary, but now we were down to just under forty boys and about twenty-five girls in the female part of the school. The cost of going to this school for the current school year had risen to $180.00 Confederate. Because the future of the Confederacy is in doubt and our dollar is so weak, the tuition is now three times the amount it was in 1861!

"Today's drill will take place at 3 o'clock. Please be sure your muskets have been cleaned well. I don't want to see any rust on your weapons due to the shower we had yesterday. Is that understood?" asked the captain.

"Yes, sir!" shouted the cadets.

The City of Tallahassee had purchased one hundred .69 caliber flintlock muskets for the military school. That was about six or seven years ago. Each cadet is issued a musket and is responsible for its upkeep. The cadet issued muskets are kept in a rack in the dormitory, and all the rest of the weapons are kept in the armory. The muskets are too big and heavy for the ten, eleven, and twelve year olds, so our "baby cadets" are issued "toy" muskets until they are strong and big enough to move up to the real thing.

"Also, Private Bryan and Private Dickson your bunks were not in order this morning, so I am giving you guard duty at the Masonic Hall, where a couple of Union prisoners are being kept. Please, report there following our afternoon drill session."

"Men, I want to remind you that if you are not shining your brass buttons or shining your boots, I want you studying your books, and studying hard! Some of you are getting behind on your studies. You know who you are. If you are having any problems with a subject, please swallow your pride and talk to a teacher about it. I don't want any of my cadets falling behind," advised Johnson.

"That concludes this morning's parade."

"Parade is dismissed!"

"Cadet Lieutenant Randolph, take charge of the men," commanded Captain Johnson.

First Lieutenant Henry Randolph was from Tallahassee and would soon turn 18 years old. All the boys looked up to him, and he made an excellent leader. Captain Johnson was a bit worried that Randolph would soon be drafted into the regular army, in spite of his still continuing to study at the military institute.

Lt. Randolph marched us to the kitchen for our breakfast. I was looking forward to some hot food, and the thought of eggs and grits made my mouth water with anticipation. Because Florida was so far from the major battlefields of the war, we were not having food shortages like folks in Virginia were.

After breakfast it was off to class. We had classes in math and chemistry taught by Mr. Melton, classes in history taught by Mr. Frazier, Christian education conducted by Rev. John DuBose, classes in English and French taught by Mr. Sartori, and military tactics taught by Captain Johnson. By the time we finished taking all our classes and drilling on the parade ground, we were all mentally and physically exhausted.

When I got back to the dorm I checked the duty roster and was happy to find my name was not on it. That meant I could relax until supper. So I sat on my bunk and read my history lesson. I read about the Punic Wars and Hannibal's fight against Rome. It was easy for me to imagine that General Lee was a modern day Hannibal fighting the might and power of Rome, or should I say Washington, DC. While I read my chapter and daydreamed, I could hear Luther up on his bunk doing something.

"Hey, Gene, are you any good with a needle? I popped off one of my jacket's pelican buttons, and I can't seem to get the darn thread through the eye of the needle. A little help, please!" Luther pleaded.

Captain Johnson went to Richmond, Virginia in the spring of 1864 to buy some new accoutrements for our uniforms. Well, one of the best things he brought back was a giant bag of Louisiana State brass buttons, you know, the ones with the pelican design. He thought the pelican was just as good a symbol for a Florida uniform as the Louisiana uniforms for which they had been intended, and besides, they were on sale. So, since last year we've had these smart looking buttons on our jackets.

"Luther, you know I'm hopeless when it comes to sewing. Why don't you get Tom Archer's sister to sew it on for you," I said.

Tom Archer had a sister in the female department of the school by the name of Susan. She was pretty, and smart to boot. When we got our new buttons last year she was one of half a dozen girls who volunteered to sew them on for us. A few of the boys did the job themselves, but most of us were only too happy to have the job done for us.

"You know, that's a good idea. I think I'll ask her when I see her at supper tonight," said Luther.

Slam! Bam!

Eddie Northrup was walking by my bunk and dropped his books by accident onto the floor. Luther and I began to laugh at him for being clumsy.

"What are ya'll laughing at?" asked Eddie with a frown.

"Oh, nothing," I said casually.

"Look, I wouldn't laugh if I was you, not with those big ears of yours. You look like an elephant!"

Edward Northrup was from a well-to-do family in Marianna. He was a big boy for just 15 years old, and had a reputation for being a bully. A couple of the other cadets liked to hang out with him, so he had his own little gang, of sorts.

"Hey, I'm sorry," I apologized.

"Well, Eugene, you best watch your step," Eddie threatened, as he collected up his books and continued on his way.

"Gene, I think Eddie has it in for you," Luther said.

I was of average height and a little on the slim side, so I have to admit that Eddie intimidated me. Was Eddie going to become a problem for me? I hoped not, but only time would tell.

12

After supper Luther and I sat on our bunks in a candle lit dormitory and shined our boots in the dim light in preparation for the next day. The war was not going well for the South and we both worried about our future. So, as we shined our boots, we discussed the latest news of the war with much apprehension.

"Luther, did you hear the news today? It came over the telegraph this afternoon." I said. "Two days ago General Sherman captured Columbia, you know, the state capital of South Carolina. Then yesterday the Yankees burnt most of the city to the ground!"

"Those Yanks have no respect for civilian property," Luther said with a sigh. "Seems like the only news we get these days is bad news."

"Yes, and I'm worried about what will happen if General Sherman's army continues north and joins forces with General Grant up in Petersburg, Virginia. I just don't think the Army of Northern Virginia will be able to hold out against Grant's and Sherman's combined forces," I admitted.

"Oh, come on, Gene! Sometimes you are such a pessimist. General Robert E. Lee can hold Richmond until the cows come home! You got to believe!!!"

Luther's positive outlook on life always made being around him a pleasure. Even when the darkest clouds of life hang over his head, he always sees a silver lining. He is a strong patriot, and has a firm faith. I felt lucky to have such a friend.

13

Because of the possibility of fire in the dormitory, every evening a cadet would perform dorm guard duties. It was only two hours long. The first shift began at 8 o'clock, with a new dorm guard every two hours after that, up to eight o'clock the next morning. This evening the name of Pvt. Eugene Murray was not on the Dorm Guard Roster, I was happy to say.

I had just finished polishing my boots when I heard the Dorm Guard coming down the hall.

As he came down the hall he called, "Lights out!"

I blew out the candle and rolled into bed. The smell of hot wax from the candle wafted through the dark room. I said my bedtime prayer and wished Luther a good night.

It had been a busy day and I welcomed sleep.

Chapter 2

"These darn skeeters!" complained Joshua, as he slapped one that had landed on his neck.

"It's February and they be comin' out already. Why, back in Virginia, where I come from, there ain't no skeeters 'til after Easter."

Joshua Jackson was a private in the 2nd Regiment U.S. Colored Infantry. Born a slave on a plantation in Stafford County, Virginia, he was freed by Union troops in 1863. Later that same year he joined the newly formed 2nd Regiment U.S. Colored Infantry at Arlington, Virginia.

"Shoot! Back in Saint Charles Parish we got skeeters big as hummingbirds!" joked Joe Henry.

Since Joe's joining the 2nd Regiment in New Orleans, in early 1864 while the 2nd was posted to that largest of southern cities, Joe and Joshua had become the closest of friends. Whereas Joshua had been treated with a degree of kindness by his master, Joe had not been so lucky. As a field hand picking cotton he had suffered often under his cruel master. Neither man could read or write, but only Joe had felt the sting of the bullwhip. Now, the 2nd gave him a family and a home. It also gave him an opportunity to prove himself a man.

"Joe, I wonder just how long we goin' to stay at this God forsaken fort in the middle of the swamp. I wish I was back with the rest of our regiment at Fort Taylor, at good ole Key West," said Joshua. "How 'bout you?"

"Oh, I liked Key West just fine, but we got us a purpose here at Fort Myers," said Joe with conviction. "Our cavalry units been raidin' the rebels' herds of cattle, and I hear we done took over three thousand head. That's a hell of a lot of meat that ain't goin' to feed those rebs up north."

During the Seminole Indian War a fort was built on the Caloosahatchie River and was named Fort Myers. The fort was abandoned when the war with the Seminoles was over. Then in 1863 the Union captured Vicksburg, cutting the Confederacy in half, and preventing Texas cattle from getting through to hungry Confederate troops in the east. Suddenly, Florida's cattle became a major source of meat for the Southern troops from Georgia to Virginia.

In early 1864, Fort Myers was reopened. It was the only U.S. Army post in peninsular Florida, and its main purpose was to be a base of operations for raiding cattle herds in central Florida. In addition to that, the fort was a haven for

Union sympathizers. At one point as many as 400 refugees were living in the fort, their homes having been burnt to the ground by secessionists.

Bang!

"What in the world was that?" asked Joe.

"I think it was the picket firing a warning shot," said Joshua.

A few moments later a bugle could be heard playing the call for assembly and shouts were heard from the parade ground.

In ran Sergeant John Fisher with a lantern in his hand, shouting, "Alright, men, accouter up! An enemy force has been spotted approaching the fort!"

Joshua grabbed his sack coat and quickly buttoned the four brass buttons. Next, he ran to the peg holding his leather accoutrements, throwing on the cartridge box and buckling up his belt, he grabbed his Springfield musket out of the gun rack, and ran out to the parade ground to fall in with the rest of his company.

The moon was nearly full and provided a fair amount of natural light that evening. Joshua could see the two companies of the 2nd Infantry Regiment formed up, and off to the left he could see the cavalry in the process of forming up. The fort had a full regiment of cavalry, and two companies of infantry, but no artillerymen had been assigned to the fort. The top brass felt that the fort would never be attacked so a company of artillerymen would be a waste of manpower. Therefore, this necessitated training some of the infantry in the art of working a field cannon. The fort had two 6 pounders and about a dozen soldiers were trained to work them.

Joshua's company commander, Captain Edward Tracy, ordered his men to the fort's parapet. They ran up the stairs and manned the fort's wall, rifles at the ready.

"You see anything, Joe?" asked Joshua.

"Nope, even with the moonlight it's just too dark,"said Joe.

Joshua thought for a moment and then said, "I wonder how the picket spotted the rebs?"

Just then, off to the east of the fort, Joshua spotted the flame from a torch, and the gleam off of a saber. Sure enough, there was someone out there, about half a mile from the fort.

"There! Did you see it, Joe! There is an enemy force out there after all!" exclaimed Joshua.

Captain Tracy ordered his men to hold their fire. Shooting into the dark would be a waste of ammo, and it was not likely that the rebels would attack at night. The good captain was 33 years old, and like all three of the officers of B Company, 2nd Regiment U.S. Colored Infantry, white. He had been a teacher back in Wilmington, Delaware before the war, and all of his company respected him greatly. He was always fair, not too hard on the men, and not too easy on them either.

The night passed without any further incident. It was quiet until dawn, then the rebs fired a warning shot from a field cannon. Next, a Confederate trooper was seen approaching the fort under a white flag of truce.

The trooper delivered a note from the Confederate commander, demanding the surrender of the fort.

A quick council of war was conducted by the top officers of the fort. They weighed the situation. It appeared that the enemy force was made up of about one thousand cavalry troops, and it was thought that they only had one field cannon with them. The fort had about an equal amount of troops, and two field cannons. Since the fort was not outnumbered, the only honorable thing to do was to fight it out. Therefore, a reply was sent back to the Confederate commander that stated, "Fort Myers will never surrender!"

The fort's commander ordered all his troops out of the fort, including his two cannons. They quickly formed up facing the enemy which was approximately 1,000 yards from the fort. The two artillery pieces were rolled to a slight rise where they had a good angle of fire.

The battle opened with the Union cannons firing at the enemy positions. Because the cannon crews were inexperienced, they were having trouble finding the range on the enemy. Most of the shots seemed to be passing harmlessly over the Confederates heads. The irony was the Confederate gun was not having much success either.

This artillery duel lasted almost two hours with little damage done on either side. Finally, the Union commander ordered his battle line forward. The dismounted cavalry was on the left and center of the battle line, while the two infantry companies made up the right wing of the Union force. As the Union soldiers advanced they could see that the Confederates had thrown up a light breastwork of cut pine to offer some protection.

The thin blue line continued to advance through the scrub pines and undergrowth of palmettos. When the men got to within 440 yards of the enemy, the order to halt was given.

The Confederates were positioned at the edge of some pines, with a large clearing before them. This was a cow meadow that was a little over a quarter mile wide, offering a clear field of fire.

The Union colonel shouted to his company commanders, "Fire by company!"

Joshua's company was the second company on the right wing of the Union line. He heard the order for the company on his right to fire, and a huge cloud of smoke erupted from their muskets.

Now Captain Tracy shouted, "Company, ready!"

"Aim!"

"Fire!!"

Every soldier in B Company pulled his trigger at the same time. BLAM! Like a crack of thunder, with a bellow of smoke rolling toward the foe, the company sent the enemy a volley of lead.

"Load!" the captain shouted.

Joshua grabbed a cartridge out of his cartridge box and bit the end of the paper off. Next, he poured the contents down his musket's barrel. He pulled his ram-rod and rammed the charge home. Out of the corner of his eye he could see his friend, Joe, doing the same. He went to his cap pouch and pulled out a brass firing cap. Quickly, he attached the cap to his rifled musket's nipple and went to the ready position, waiting for the next order. He did all of this in just 22 seconds!

From behind B Company Captain Tracy could see that all rifles were now loaded.

He shouted, "Fire by file, starting on the right."

"Commence firing!"

A battle line was made up of two ranks, a front rank and a rear rank. The first file on the far right of the company was made up of the First Corporal in the front rank and the man behind him in the rear rank. At the command, "Commence firing", the two men in the first file fired their muskets, then the next two men to their left fired, then the next two men fired, and so on, all the way down the company line.

When the company had finished firing by files, the captain gave the order to "Fire at will!"

Each man in the company fired at the enemy at his own pace, with a little more time devoted to aiming.

Joshua could see puffs of smoke coming from the enemy positions. Each time a rebel soldier fired his weapon he exposed his head and shoulders above the breastworks. Joshua tried to time his firing to catch the rebs as they came up to take a shot at him and his fellow soldiers. He could hear bullets whizzing by his ears from time to time. Surely it was a miracle that no one in his company had been hit so far.

This exchange of fire continued for quite some time. Finally, the order to cease fire could be heard up and down the battle line.

The colonel shouted the order, "Forward, March!"

At that order the color guard advanced six paces ahead of the battle line. The color guard consisted of one standard bearer with the Star Spangled Banner, and an armed man on each side of him with the purpose of protecting the flag.

Captain Tracy moved to a position about six paces ahead of B Company and each of the company captains could be seen to be doing the same. He held his sword horizontally with both hands while facing his company and walking backwards toward the enemy. His job was to keep his company aligned with the rest of the battle line, making sure that B Company neither pulled ahead nor lagged behind the rest of the line.

Keeping the battle line straight was a challenge. Sergeant Fisher was heard several times to remind the men to, "Dress it up!"

After the Union line had advanced about one hundred yards, the order to halt was given. Now there were less than three hundred yards between the opposing sides, and the rebels kept up a steady stream of fire. The rebels were not regular army. They consisted of cowboys whose job was to herd cattle, and because beef for the Confederate army was so vital, they were exempt from army service. However, the raids coming from Fort Myers were beginning to really hurt the rebels, so they organized a regiment of cavalry, calling themselves the "Cow Cavalry". This was the force that was opposing the Union line.

"Fire at will!" Captain Tracy shouted.

Joshua kept up a steady rate of fire. He checked his cartridge box and discovered he was nearly out of ammo in the top portion of his box. Quickly he moved cartridges from the bottom of his tin to the top portion. It was while he was busy doing this that the man on the other side of Joe, Nehemiah Brooks, suddenly lurched forward and fell to the ground. The man clutched at his right thigh, and a scarlet stain began to grow on his breaches.

"Nehemiah, what happened?" asked Joe Henry.

Nehemiah had joined the regiment at about the same

time as Joe did. Although he had a stutter, he was very popular with everyone in the company. There was a grimace on the man's face, and he must have been in considerable pain.

"Joe, I's shot in de leg. C-c-can you help me to de rear?" asked Nehemiah.

Joe grounded his musket and helped the wounded man to his feet. They passed through the line where Joe sat Nehemiah down a few yards behind the battle line. Then Joe pulled a large handkerchief from his haversack and tied it around Nehemiah's leg. He placed his hand on the wound and pressed with a steady pressure stemming the flow of blood.

"I ain't no doctor but I don't think the bullet hit yo' thigh bone," Joe said.

"Dat be g-g-good news," Nehemiah stuttered.

Captain Tracy came over and looked at the situation. "Can you walk, Private Brooks?"

"Yes, sir, captain. I think so."

"Alright then, Private Henry, I want you to take him back to the fort," the captain said. "It's only about half a mile, and there Doc Wilson can fix him up."

Nehemiah leaned on Joe as they worked their way back to the fort. The sounds of battle slowly softened with every step they took away from the melee. At about a quarter mile from the fort one of the cannon crew came forward to offer a hand. Now with a strong man on each side of him, Nehemiah quickly finished the trek to get medical help. While he received help from the doctor, the battle raged on.

The Confederates didn't want to give up their defensive position, so they waited for a grand Federal attack which never came. The Union colonel felt that all he needed to do to win the battle was remain in possession of the field. He thought it would be a waste of good men to mount a direct attack on the Confederates. So the battle continued in a stale-mate fashion, with both sides gradually running low on ammunition.

"Cease fire!" was shouted by the company commanders. "Cease fire!"

"Kneel!"

Several men were sent back to the fort to bring up boxes of much needed ammo. The Union force waited patiently for their return.

The Confederates stopped firing as well and, for a half hour, both sides just stared at each other across that three hundred yard gap. The men of B Company opened their haversacks and pulled out some hardtack during the lull. This was the first food they had enjoyed all day, since the battle had begun before they could get their breakfast that morning. Although the hardtack was difficult to eat, the men gnawed on it with relish.

At last the men returned with wooden boxes of paper cartridges. The ammunition was quickly distributed to all of the troops.

"Rise!" shouted Captain Tracy.

"Load!"

"Fire by company!" ordered the colonel.

Once again the company on the right of B Company could be seen to aim their rifles and fire at the command. A cloud of smoke rolled toward the enemy.

"Company, ready!" shouted Captain Tracy.

"Aim!"

"Fire!"

The volley was fired in complete unison as every man pulled his trigger at the same instant.

"Fire at will!" ordered the captain.

A steady stream of fire was being exchanged between the Union and Confederate forces. Joshua couldn't tell if the rebels were taking any hits, but he felt that surely with all the lead being poured into their position, they must be. The battle had been going on for hours and Joshua was beginning to sweat in spite of the chilly afternoon.

While Joshua was ramming his ram-rod down the barrel of his musket in preparation to fire his next shot, the Confederates fired a mass volley with a huge cloud of smoke obscuring them from view. A moment later Joshua saw two men in the line fall forward. One of the men shot was the color corporal to the right of the standard bearer. He was clearly dead, having been shot through the forehead. It was not a pretty sight. He was face down and much of the back of his head had been blown off. Joshua thought to himself, it's a good thing he had skipped breakfast or that meal would have come up about now.

The other man was one of the cavalrymen in the center part of the battle line. He had been shot in the shoulder and it looked like he might survive.

And so it went. The winter sun began to dip low into the sky. Neither side moved.

Finally, as the pale sun began to drop behind the pines, the rebels could be seen pulling out. They must have been low or out of ammo by now and retreat was their only option.

The Union colonel did not feel it wise to pursue the enemy. His men had stood firm, and he was proud to say, they had possession of the battlefield at the end of the day. The victory was theirs and Union casualties had been light.

This was Joshua's first battle. He had been scared, yet he had stood with his comrades during the thickest part of the fight. Yes, indeed, he had "seen the elephant", and lived to tell the tale.

Chapter 3

"Gene, wake up!" Luther said.

I opened my eyes, stretched my arms, and gave a long yawn. It was Sunday morning and on Sundays the color ceremony was half an hour later than usual, giving us a chance to sleep in a little bit. Once we got colors out of the way, the day was all ours to do with as we liked. Yes, it was the one day of the week we could actually relax.

Being Sunday, all of the stores in Tallahassee were closed, so shopping was not an option, but there were many ways to enjoy the day. Most of the cadets would go to morning worship service at one of the town churches. Then, after lunch, they might play baseball, horseshoes, or go fishing in one of the many county lakes.

I had been going to the Methodist church with Luther most Sundays, but my family was Presbyterian, so I thought maybe I should try Tallahassee's Presbyterian Church. The Presbyterian Church was a beautiful white Greek Revival church built in 1838. It was located at the corner of McCarty and Adams Street, only about five blocks from the seminary. It was the most impressive church in the capital city.

So, after morning colors and breakfast, Luther and I walked up the hill to our respective churches.

"Don't worry about waiting for me after church, I'm not sure when the Presbyterian pastor will finish his sermon," I told Luther. I bid him adieu as he went into the Methodist church while I continued up McCarty to the stately white church with the four grand columns.

People dressed in their Sunday best were entering the church. At the door of the church I was greeted by a gentleman in a frock coat and top hat. "Good morning! Welcome to the Presbyterian Church," he said with a smile.

I went a little way down the left aisle and set down in one of the pews. All the pews were painted white with black trim. There were four white columns on each side of the sanctuary supporting an upstairs gallery. I could see that colored folk were sitting up there.

In the pew ahead of me sat three individuals, a gentleman in frock coat with a goatee, his wife in a lovely gray with white polka dot dress, and his daughter in a pretty blue plaid dress with navy blue bonnet.

The kind gentleman turned to me and asked, "Are you new here?"

"Yes, sir, this is my first time here," I replied.

"May I introduce myself? I am Mr. James MacLaren, owner of the bookstore on Monroe Street. This is my wife, Mrs.

Beth MacLaren, and my daughter, Miss Jenny MacLaren.

Miss MacLaren turned and gave me a smile that just melted my heart. She was a lovely girl with fair skin, blond hair and blue eyes. Her nose was a little long, but it just added character to her face.

"I'm Eugene Murray of Monticello, and as you can see from my uniform I am a cadet from the Florida Military Institute."

Since the beginning of the war many people were calling the West Florida Seminary, the Florida Military Institute. However, for some reason Governor Milton did not like the name and refused to make it official.

"Well, Cadet Murray, we are happy to have you visit our church today," said Mr. MacLaren.

The church was filling up pretty quickly now, and I saw Reverend John DuBose in a black robe with white collar walk up the right aisle and take his seat in a large chair next to the pulpit. I glanced up and to the right and could see the colored folk up in the gallery.

"Mr. MacLaren, could you tell me about the gallery, please?" I asked.

"Our church is concerned for the souls of all men, regardless of race. So we encourage all of our members who own slaves to bring them to church so that they may participate in the worship experience. As you can see, the gallery is reserved for our colored people and it is full," he said.

Now the choir filed in taking their seats in the rear of the nave.

Rev. DuBose began the worship service with a long prayer. He prayed for all the sick members of the church, then he prayed for Governor Milton, for President Jefferson Davis, and for General Robert E. Lee, that the Lord grant them wisdom and strength to carry on the fight.

The first hymn we sang was one of my favorites, "Love Divine, All Loves Excelling". While we sang this hymn I noticed Jenny give me a couple of sideway glances. Could she possibly think I was handsome? Anyway, I thought she was quite comely.

The pastor gave an interesting sermon on Paul's debate with the Athenian philosophers on the Areopagus hill in Athens. He said that the Greek philosophers believed that the life unexamined is not worth living. That made me look at my life thus far, and wonder what purpose God had for my future. Was I just wandering through life like a blind man, like so many other people? No, in my heart I knew that the hand of Providence was guiding me down life's path.

When the service was over we all began to file out of the church. The MacLaren family was right behind me.

"Oh, papa, can we invite the cadet to lunch?" Miss MacLaren asked her father.

He thought for a second, then asked, "Beth, will there be enough for a guest?"

"Oh, heavens, that's no problem," his wife replied.

Outside the church Mr. MacLaren invited me to have lunch with his family if I didn't have any plans already. Of course I jumped at the chance to spend some time with his lovely daughter, and get a home cooked meal as well!

"Our home is only about two and a half blocks away, and on a mild day like today it will be a pleasant stroll," said Mr. MacLaren.

He offered his arm to his wife and they began the walk side by side home. A cool breeze suddenly began to blow and Miss MacLaren pulled her dark blue shawl a bit closer. Being the gentleman that I am, I offered my arm to the lovely young lady, which she accepted with a smile as we promenaded down McCarty.

Mr. MacLaren explained that in 1855 he purchased his bookstore on Monroe Street. A couple of years later he had made enough money selling books to have a small cottage built on the north side of McCarty, right across the street from the Murphy house.

He lit a cigar, and then asked, "Do you know what this street was called back in the territorial days?"

"No, sir."

"Well, they used to call it 200 Foot Street. That's because when the town of Tallahassee was laid out in the 1820s, the town had a 200 foot wide dirt road all the way around it. This was so that the Indians could not sneak up on the town and, should the town need to be defended, it gave a clear field of fire," he explained.

"Also, we had a terrible fire back in 1843. There was a south wind blowing on that day in May and the fire started in Washington Hall, across the street from the Capitol. There were many wooden stores and warehouses in the early days of downtown Tallahassee, and the fire swept north through the town like a cyclone from Hell, devouring everything in its path. But, when it got to 200 Foot Street it couldn't leap the 200 foot barrier, the street was a natural fire break."

"Sir, is that why you built your house on the north side of the street?"

"Yes, that, and the property was cheaper," he said with a chuckle.

Miss MacLaren chimed in with, "But, papa, McCarty is so very boring. I think we should plant some trees down the middle of it. What do you think, Cadet Murray?"

"Oh, please call me Gene, all my friends do.

"And by all means, please call me Jenny," replied Miss MacLaren.

Yes, I like your idea of planting trees down the middle of McCarty Street," I said thoughtfully. "Some day it would be a lovely boulevard."

As we crossed Calhoun Street I saw the most beautiful Greek Revival two-story house on the south-east corner. The house was painted white with dark green shutters, and had four grand columns out front.

"Whose fancy house is that?" I asked.

"Oh, that belongs to the widow Catherine Hagner. Her husband, Tom, was a local attorney who gave her the house as a wedding gift. Sadly, he passed away some time ago and now it's a boarding house."

"I believe the house was built by George Proctor. Mr. Proctor, a free colored man, built many of the finest homes in Tallahassee. Unfortunately, he caught the gold bug and rushed off to California during the Gold Rush days, never to return to town," he explained.

We walked up to a handsome cottage, painted in a lovely sky blue with white trim. Mr. MacLaren opened the gate to the white picket fence and we filed down the garden path to the front door.

"Gene, why don't we sit in the parlor while the ladies

prepare our dinner?"

The parlor was a cozy room. It had a fireplace with a mantel, and on top of the mantel was a fine old clock that chimed on the hour. There were a couple of upholstered chairs and a nice sofa. On one wall was a bookcase full of old books. In the middle of the room was a small table with a kerosene lamp.

I took a seat on the sofa, while Mr. MacLaren sat in one of the chairs smoking his cigar. He asked me about my family, and I told him that unfortunately I was an only child. My father was a deputy for the sheriff of Jefferson County, and my parents wanted me to get a good education at West Florida Seminary.

About that time, Jenny popped her head in the door and said, "Pa, tell Gene about the Ring Tournament you helped organize."

"Well, now, that is an interesting story," he said with a grin.

"Back in the 1850s chivalry was alive and well in Tallahassee. Yes, starting in 1851 and lasting until the war began, Ring Tournaments were very popular here in the capital city."

"Pardon my ignorance, but what is a ring tournament?" I asked.

"Have you ever read the book, Ivanhoe, by Sir Walter Scott?"

"Yes, sir, it's one of my favorites," I admitted.

"Well, that novel fired the imaginations of many Southern gentlemen, with its colorful jousting scenes between Saxon and Norman knights. So it was only natural that a group of young gentlemen should want to mimic the excitement of the Tilt. The tournament was a contest to see who, or rather which "knight", was the best horsemen in the area. During the 1850s it became the rage, and the winner got to crown his favorite lady 'The Queen of Love and Beauty'."

"The Ring Tournaments were part of the George Washington's Birthday celebrations each February during the '50s. They were held in a grassy glen just off of the road to Thomasville, a little bit north of town. The lancers had to ride at full gallop down a 200 yard course. In the middle of the course hung an ivory ring from a hook, and the rider had to slip the ring from the hook onto his lance. Each "knight" got three tries, and the one with the most rings won the tournament."

"In February 1854 I helped to organize that year's Ring Tournament. I was the Judge of Sport, or rather the fellow who would award the winner the crown for his lady."

"Now, each young gentleman took on the personality of a knight of yore. There were ten young men who rode in that year's contest and they were as follows: The Knight of St. Johns, the Knight of Jefferson, the Knight of Monteith, the Knight of the White Plume, the Knight of the Highlands, the Knight of Aucilla, the Knight of the Forest, the Black Knight, the Knight of the Lake, and the Knight of the Falcon."

"On the night before the contest northern Florida had a hard freeze, but in spite of the cold morning many spectators came out to watch the contest which began at 11 o'clock."

"Each knight took a turn at trying to snare the ivory ring and the crowd witnessed a terrible spill on the first run of the Black Knight. He had just missed the ring with his lance and he pulled the lance and reins back too fast as he passed the target, jerking the horses head. At the same moment, the horse slipped on a patch of ice, which caused the horse to do a somersault. The crowd gasped in fear for the rider's life as horse and rider hit the ground with a crash, but the gentleman walked away from the accident with just a slight limp. And, miraculously, the horse trotted off without injury."

"At the beginning of the second run the Knight of St. Johns had problems with his horse. He spurred it, but the stallion refused to start. Finally, he got it to charge down the course, but just as he was approaching the ring his horse pulled up three or four yards short of the goal. Embarrassed, the knight with head hung low, slowly crept off the field."

"By the end of the third run there was a three way tie between the Knight of Monteith, the Knight of the White Plume, and the Knight of St. Johns. As Judge of Sport, I decreed that in all fairness the Knight of St. Johns should have another run allowed. All of the knights agreed that this was the only fair and proper thing to do."

"So, the Knight of St. Johns made his run, but as he approached the ring, he slowed to a trot and intentionally knocked the ring off, forfeiting his chance of victory."

"The crowd roared their approval!! It was a most noble act of chivalry."

"In the end the Knight of Monteith won the Ring Tournament. When he walked his steed up to the judge's chair, I placed the victor's crown on the tip of his lance. He then trotted twice around the grassy bowl, finally stopping in front of the lovely Virginia Wright and presented her with the crown, making her the Queen of Love and Beauty."

"That night a Fancy Ball was held at the Capitol building where the Knight of Monteith and his queen sat upon their thrones. It was a wonderful night of ladies in hoop-skirted ball gowns, whirling with their gentlemen to the rhythm and flow of the waltz," said Mr. MacLaren.

"Shucks! I wish I could be in a tournament like that! It would be so exciting!" I exclaimed.

"Yes, well, someday this war will come to an end, and perhaps the Ring Tournaments will return," he replied.

Jenny, wearing an apron, came to the parlor door. "Dinner is ready," she said.

We all retired to the dining room where I was pleased to see a delicious meal spread out on the table. There was a big smoked ham, collard greens, butter beans, and corn bread. It smelled divine.

After we were all seated, Mr. MacLaren said grace.

Jenny sat straight across the table from me and I was mesmerized by her charm. She was intelligent and possessed all of the virtues of a lady; she had poise, grace, but most important of all, I could tell she had a kind heart. Oh, and one more thing, she had a sense of humor.

I turned to Mrs. MacLaren and said, "please pardon me for not eating any of your butter beans, but you see, at the seminary we eat beans for almost every meal, and if I eat just one more bean I will turn into a GIANT BEAN!!!"

Everyone laughed at that!

The MacLaren's hospitality was making me feel right at home. Between the delicious meal and the opportunity to converse with a lovely and charming angel, surely I was in paradise.

As I was finishing the last of my ham, Jenny asked, "Gene, do you know how to play whist?"

"Well, I've played it a couple of times. Why?"

"You need four people to play and usually there is just the three of us," she said.

"Mama, can we put off washing the dishes until Gene leaves? It would be so much fun for all of us to play a game of whist, don't you think?" asked Jenny.

"I Suwannee! Child, you would do anything to get out of doing work. But, it's not everyday we have a visitor, so yes, as soon as we clear off the dishes we can play a hand of whist."

The dishes were quickly cleared away, and a pack of cards placed on the table.

Rather than draw cards to determine partners, Mr. and Mrs. MacLaren said they would volunteer to be one team, and their daughter and I could be the other. That sounded just perfect to me.

I must confess I prefer playing checkers to playing cards, but with Jenny as my partner I was having loads of fun playing whist. And, by Jiminy, it must have been beginners luck, Jenny and I reached seven points first, winning the game! Mind you, Jenny, won most of our tricks, and if it had not been for her skill, I'm mighty sure my team would have lost. Anyway, I had a wonderful time.

"It's getting late, and I must be on my way back to the seminary," I said as I grabbed my kepi from the hat rack.

"We must have a re-match on the whist game next time

you come," Mr. MacLaren said as he shook my hand.

"Ya'll have been so nice. Mrs. MacLaren, thank you for the delicious dinner. Good-bye," I said and headed back to the school.

When I got back to the dorm Luther was waiting for me.

"Where have you been all afternoon?" Luther wanted to know.

"Luther, I met the nicest family at church today, and they invited me home for dinner. And, better yet, their daughter would rival Helen of Troy for looks and charm. It was a most enjoyable day!"

"Well, my friend, we have a lot of cleaning to do to get our room into shape for tomorrow's room inspection," Luther commented. "And, I recommend we get started soon."

We dusted the room, swept the floor, mopped the floor, polished the brass door knob, shined our boots, and did all the things a cadet was expected to do before turning in for the night.

"Oh, and Gene, don't forget that you have Dorm Guard duty from mid-night until 2 o'clock," Luther reminded me.

"Thanks, buddy, and good night," I said with a yawn. The Dorm Guard would wake me when it was time for me to take over, and with that thought I fell into a deep sleep.

Chapter 4

"Joe, the Magnolia just came in and I overheard its captain tell Major Weeks that General Newton is plannin' something big. Something about us goin' to St. Marks and us shuttin' down that haven for blockade runners," Joshua said.

"Sho' 'nough?" asked Joe.

"That's what I heard," Joshua continued. "And the captain also told about pickin' up some refugees. While on his way here he was passin' a small island about 20 miles south of Punta Rassa and saw a white flag, so he sent a party ashore to take a closer look. There was a cracker woman with her six children and they were half starved."

"Then all of a sudden they hear gun shots. They look where the shots be comin' from and see two white men swimmin' across the narrow strait, and on the shore a small group of men firing pistols at them. That's when the landin' party opened up with their rifles and the Rebels ran for the woods! Unfortunately, one of the two men that be swimmin' got himself shot in the arm and he drowned about half way across. The other made it to shore, though."

In the last year of the war Governor Milton ordered all white men in the State of Florida between the ages of 18 and 55 to either join the regular Confederate army or join the militia, the home guard. Conscription officers rode around the state enforcing this law. They had a roster of the names of the men serving in the army and when they came to a homestead that wasn't on their list they forced the men there into joining their ranks. However, if they found no men at home, it was assumed the men had gone into hiding, and they burned the home to the ground, leaving the family to fend for them- selves.

With General Sherman burning a path through Georgia, and now the Carolinas, and with a blockade that tightens more and more with each month that passes, the war was going very badly for the South. The first major port in the South to fall to Union forces was New Orleans in April 1862, and then in August of 1864 the port of Mobile, Alabama fell. The Federal blockade put the final nail in the coffin when the last major port of Wilmington, North Carolina fell to the Union in January 1865.

And then on top of that, desertion was becoming a major problem in the Confederate army, and finding new recruits was a huge challenge. Some men just wanted to be left alone to take care of their family; they didn't see any point in fighting for a lost cause, or they may have harbored sympathies for the Union. This attitude resulted in many homesteads being burnt to the ground by Conscription officers in the last months of the war. The Union army posts from Fort Pickens to Cedar Key to Fort Myers were filling up with refugees seeking food and shelter.

While Joshua and Joe were talking this over, in came Sgt. Fisher with some important news.

"Men, we got orders to move out! Colonel Townsend and the rest of the regiment is waiting for us at Cedar Key, and we are to depart as soon as our transports come in," said the sergeant.

"How much time do we have, sergeant?" asked Joshua.

"Well, according to Captain Chatfield of the Magnolia, two transports should arrive this very afternoon. So we don't have much time. We need to get all of our equipment together fast."

For the next couple of hours there was a flurry of activity in B Company. Joshua and Joe went to the Quartermaster and were issued everything they would need for the next week, and then they carefully packed it all into their knapsacks and haversacks.

About the time they were nearly finished with their packing, the Honduras and the Hussar came in and docked. The men, their equipment, and two field cannons were quickly loaded on board the transports. With just over an hour and a half of daylight left the expedition headed down the Caloosahatchee River.

Soon after sailing into the Gulf of Mexico the small fleet turned north to follow the coast to Cedar Key. There was a fair breeze blowing as the sun lowered itself onto the horizon.

While most of B Company was below, Joshua and Joe had stayed with a small group up on deck where they were leaning on the port railing and admiring the scenery. The men watched a huge red ball of fire slip into the deep blue sea, with a few wispy pink clouds floating in the sky. It was like something you might see in an oil painting, and the men were mesmerized by it.

"Josh, ain't that the most beautiful sunset you ever did see?" asked Joe.

"Just beautiful," Joshua replied.

A seaman came over to the small group and in a friendly voice inquired, "Where you boys from?"

"Most of us is from Virginia, and the rest is from Louisiana," volunteered Corporal Andy Bates. "How 'bout yourself?"

"Oh, I'm from a small seafaring town in Connecticut called Mystic," said the red bearded seaman.

"That's a strange name for a town," said Joshua.

"So it is," said the sailor. "But, it's a town with a great whaling tradition, and from the time I was a young lad all I ever wanted to do was go to sea."

"I'll bet you've got a story or two to tell," said Joe.

"Well, let's see now. Do you want a tale of pretty mermaids and horrible sea monsters, or something that really happened?"

The men all had a good laugh.

"Give us a real story, if you don't mind," said Corporal Bates.

The sailor thought for a second while scratching his beard. "Before I was assigned to the Honduras, I was on the U.S.S. Huron, a blockading cruiser with orders to patrol the approaches to Wilmington, North Carolina, along with about three dozen other blockade ships."

"On a cloudless morning in August of 1863 we spotted a steam ship on the horizon heading south, possibly heading for Nassau in the Bahamas. We put on all of our sail and the race was on."

"Many hours passed and we could tell we were very gradually gaining on the steamer. By mid-afternoon we were within four miles of the blockade runner, when suddenly the ship began to emit a cloud of very black smoke, and it increased its speed. It took us a while to figure out what they were up to, but finally the First Mate said he knew what was happening; they were burning cotton drenched in turpentine."

"At twilight a fog bank could be seen moving in from the southeast, and the enemy ship headed straight for it. It disappeared into the fog soon after and we never saw that ship again."

"A week later I read in the newspaper the story of how the C.S.S. Robert E. Lee had run the blockade by using cotton soaked in turpentine for an explosive fuel. I'm sure that was the ship that eluded us, and no wonder we couldn't catch her, she was using a secret weapon," said the sailor with a wink.

By now it was completely dark and beginning to get chilly. A steady breeze was blowing out of the south, enabling the small fleet to move quickly up the west coast of Florida. Thousands of stars twinkled in the night sky, and a moon that was three quarters full slowly rose reflecting off the water with an eerie illumination.

"The night is still young; you got another story?" asked Andy. Then he added, "Oh, did your ship ever catch any blockade runners?"

"Well, now, during the eighteen months I was on the Huron we only captured one blockade runner," replied the sailor. "It was the Cambria, a British ship that was attempting to run into Charleston harbor. We caught it just south of Sullivan's Island before it could reach the safety of Fort Moultrie's guns. And, what a prize it was! It was carrying cases and cases of Enfield rifles, good quality wool cloth for uniform jackets and brass buttons, things the Confederacy needed badly."

"Also, we very nearly captured the C.S.S. Tallahassee, a Confederate raider."

"Tell us about that one," said Joshua.

The red haired seaman pulled out a pipe and a bag of tobacco. After stuffing the tobacco into the bowl, he struck a match and lit the pipe, blowing a large cloud of smoke into the night air.

"It was back last August. We were on blockade patrol about 30 miles southeast of the mouth of the Cape Fear River, the river that Wilmington, North Carolina is on, when the U.S.S. Nansemond signaled that we were to follow her north in pursuit of an enemy ship. That ship was the Confederate raider, C.S.S. Tallahassee, which had just eluded our blockade with her speed and was last seen headed north up the coast."

The sailor continued, "We sailed north and put into New York City's harbor. There we found out that for the last two days the raider had preyed on ships coming and going into

New York City. In that short time the Confederate raider had sunk or captured 13 ships!"

"We received orders to continue north in pursuit of the raider, and departed at dawn the next day. Sixteen more Yankee ships were sunk off the New England coast by the raider in the time it took us to reach Boston, but now she was getting low on coal and she headed for Halifax, Nova Scotia, a neutral port."

"When we got to Halifax we dropped anchor at the mouth of Halifax Bay. We were two highly armed warships against one fast but lightly armed ship, it only carried three cannons, and we had it bottled up. Surely she was ours!"

"Our captain got word from the port authorities that the rebel raider was staying for two days during which it would coal up and fix a busted mast. So, we didn't expect to see any action for a while, and turned in for a good nights sleep."

"Little did we know," the seaman smirked, "that the raider had paid the best local pilot to guide her out by using a little known route on the far side of McNab Island, in a very, very narrow channel on the east side of the bay. Early the next morning our captain was surprised to find no trace of the enemy ship with his spy glass. They had escaped during the night! Unbelievable!"

"Some of those rebel captains can be mighty crafty," said Joshua.

Captain Tracy walked over to the small knot of men.

"Attention!" called out Corporal Andy Bates when he saw the captain approach.

The men snapped to attention.

"As you were," said the captain. Most of the men leaned back onto the railing in a relaxed posture.

"How are you men doing?" asked the captain.

"Good, sir," said Joshua.

"Look, I think you men should know there is a rumor that General Newton is planning not only to take St. Marks, but also capture the state capital of Tallahassee. It could mean a promotion for him if he succeeds," Captain Tracy explained.

"Sir, will we have enough men to do that?" asked Cpl. Bates.

"If we don't meet too much opposition, yes," said the captain. "Now it's starting to get late and we have a busy day tomorrow, so I think we should all get some sleep."

"Yes, sir, good night," said several men in unison.

The men went below where there were enough hammocks strung up to accommodate the whole company. Joshua climbed into a very low slung hammock and Joe into the one above it. Some of the men were already asleep, lulled into that dream state by the gentle rocking of the ship.

"Josh, you asleep?" Joe asked.

"Nope, whatcha want?" replied Joshua.

"After the war is over, whatcha going to do?"

"Well, I'd like to go back to Virginia and buy a small farm. And I'd like to find me a good wife and have a mess of youngins," reflected Joshua.

"That sounds mighty fine. When I go back to Louisiana there's a pretty girl by the name of Pearl I'd like to look up," said Joe.

"Pearl is a pretty name," replied Joshua.

"I met her in the French Quarter of New Orleans. She's a maid in a hotel there. Dang, what a lovely face she has," Joe said with a sigh.

There was silence for a minute.

"And another thing, I don't know my birthday," said Joe out of the blue.

"Yeah, me too. I wish my massa had thought it important enough to write it down, but he didn't," said Joshua with disappointment in his voice.

"Havin' no birthday is like havin' no Christmas, it just ain't right," Joe protested.

"Yeah, well, maybe dis war will put an end to slavery, and our people will be treated like humans instead of cattle some day," replied Joshua.

"We can hope," Joe said with a yawn.

The men drifted off to sleep to the sounds of the ship's creaking, and a chorus of snoring.

By noon the next day the small fleet came into sight of the little group of islands known as the Cedar Keys. General Newton was on the Magnolia and he wanted all three ships to dock so that the men would have a chance to stretch their legs. The Magnolia and Honduras docked without incident, however, the Hussar ran aground because its pilot was inexperienced.

A couple of hours passed before high tide and there was enough water under the keel to float the Hussar. The ship then proceeded up the channel and docked with the other ships, allowing the men to disembark at the army camp on Depot Key.

General John Newton called an officers meeting after everyone was on the key. The meeting was held in the camp Headquarters tent, a very large wall tent.

"Gentlemen, I've called this meeting to explain the objectives of this expedition, and to give you an idea of the overall plan I have developed," said the general. "First of all, after we leave the Cedar Keys we will proceed to Lighthouse Point and rendezvous with several warships. Captain Chatfield, since you have a good knowledge of the coast of Florida, I want you to pilot our ships into position to launch the invasion force."

"Yes, sir," the captain replied.

"We will land at the St. Marks Lighthouse, then proceed across the East River Bridge. From there we will march north up the St. Marks River and cross the bridge at Newport. Once on the west side of the river we will continue on to Tallahassee, capturing the state capital, and bringing Florida back into the Union."

"Huzzah!!!" cheered several of the junior officers.

"Next, from Tallahassee we will march northeast to Thomasville, Georgia, where it is reported that some Union prisoners are being kept. After freeing those men, we will return to Tallahassee, holding and occupying the capital for the Union," General Newton explained.

"Are there any questions?" asked the general.

The officers looked at each other, but no one said anything. Finally, Colonel Townsend asked, "when do you want us to embark and sail for St. Marks?"

"I would like us to leave at dawn tomorrow. Captain Chatfield will pilot our ships down the channel," said the general.

"Sir, there is a problem with that, at dawn tomorrow the channel will be at ebb-tide and we may run aground," replied the captain. "However, if we wait until around noon the gulf will be at high tide."

"Very well, gentlemen we shall depart at 11 o'clock tomorrow morning. Please see to your troops and have them on board the ships by mid-morning. Thank you, and you are dismissed," said the general.

"Alright, B Company, fall in!" shouted First Sgt. Fisher.

The men formed up two ranks, and waited for their captain. Soon after, Captain Tracy arrived.

"Sergeant, are all the men accounted for?" the captain asked.

"Yes, sir, all present and accounted for," replied Sgt. Fisher.

"Attention, company!" Captain Tracy commanded.

"Right face, forward march," Captain Tracy and First Sgt Fisher took the lead in the column, and the company marched to the wharf.

The men filed up the gang-plank. Sgt. Fisher directed them to go below deck. By 11 o'clock the ship was weighing anchor and headed down the channel for the open waters of the Gulf of Mexico.

The invasion fleet was on its way to a date with destiny.

Chapter 5

*I*t was late one evening toward the end of February, less than an hour before lights out. I had finished my homework and was shining my boots when Cadet Lt. Byrd Coles came by to see me. Second Lieutenant Coles was a senior classmen, liked by everyone, and good at his studies. All the girls in town thought he was the most handsome, dashing and debonair cadet at the seminary. They loved his long sideburns and charming manner.

"Gene, how would you like to play a game of chess with me?" asked Coles.

"How do these boots look to you?" I asked.

"They look just fine, now come on over to my room and prepare to meet your defeat," he replied.

"We'll see about that!" I told him as we walked down the hall to his dorm room.

In his room I saw a table with a nice wooden chess set sitting on it. A chair and a wooden cracker box were set up next to the table, and the room was lit up by a kerosene lantern.

"Gene, you can have the chair, and I'll sit on the box," said Byrd Coles.

Luther and a few other boys crowded into the room to watch the chess game.

Well, I was doing just fine for about half an hour, and then I made a major blunder and Byrd captured my queen. Ouch!

Not too long after my mistake I heard those dreaded words that every chess player fears, 'check mate'. I knew my chances of beating Byrd had been small, yet I had hoped for success. Oh well, not tonight.

"Lieutenant, you're a tough opponent to beat. That was a good game," I congratulated him.

"Yes, thanks for the game," Coles replied.

"Come on, Luther, its nearly time for lights out," I said.

When we got back to our room Luther climbed into the upper bunk, and as usual I went over to our table and blew out the candle. I crawled into my bunk bed, but as I pushed my legs under my blanket and sheets I ran into a little problem. I couldn't stretch out. Somebody had short sheeted my bunk while I was playing chess!!! Boy was I mad!

"Dog gone it!" I swore.

I heard some boys down the hall laughing.

"What's the matter?" asked Luther.

"Oh, someone's played a little joke on me. Unless I'm going to sleep all curled up in a ball, I'm going to have to

51

remake my bunk. Sorry, buddy, but I got to light the candle so I can see what I'm doing," I told him.

I lit the candle and remade my bunk as quickly as I could, all the while wondering who had done such a thing. The only name that came to mind was Eddie Northrup. Yes, it had to be. I'll bet Eddie put Byrd Coles up to distracting me while he played his prank.

"Gene, that was a dirty trick they played on you," consoled Luther.

"No big deal," I said, "Good night pal."

I woke a few minutes before the Dorm Guard came around to wake us up. Maybe it was a rooster crowing from a farm house west of the campus. I'm not sure, but something woke me up right in the middle of an interesting dream.

Like most dreams, it was a bit crazy, for I dreamed that Jenny MacLaren was a Confederate spy in Virginia and had been captured by the Yankees. A troop of twenty Union cavalry was escorting her to Fairfax Courthouse. Jenny was riding in a black open air carriage drawn by two chestnut colored horses. And now for the surprising part, next to her was sitting none other than Napoleon Bonaparte!!!

This is where I came into the picture. For in my dream I was Colonel Eugene Murray, leader of a band of brave partisans, and the Yanks had nicknamed me the "Black Fox", because of the black plume I wore in my cavalry hat, and the fact that I always out-smarted them.

The Union party was heading northeast up the Warrenton Turnpike. My band of rangers was hiding in a group of trees just to the north of the turnpike and not far from the stone bridge that goes over Bull Run Creek. We had with us a small mountain howitzer that we had captured a couple of weeks ago. Most of the escorting cavalry unit was leading the carriage, and as they came abreast of us we fired grapeshot into the leading troopers, taking out half a dozen with that one shot.

Then we charged!

We gave them the rebel yell! "Yeehaw!!!"

With pistols and sabers drawn, we tore into the Yanks. As I shot one Yank in the chest, the trooper next to him took a shot at me. I felt the bullet graze my left shoulder. It furrowed a two inch cut in the jacket. Before he could get another shot off I shot him between the eyes and he fell dead from his horse. Meanwhile, the rest of the Union troopers were overwhelmed. The survivors took flight, riding their horses with reckless abandon to escape my men.

I trotted over to the carriage, doffed my hat, and said, "I am Colonel Murray, the Black Fox, at your service, madam. And aren't you the famous Confederate spy, Jenny MacLaren?"

"Why, yes," she said while batting her eyelashes, "and thank you ever so much for rescuing me."

"Bless my soul! Is this the famous Napoleon sitting next to you?" I asked in total astonishment.

"Oui, monsieur. I am Emperor Napoleon," he replied.

"Sir, it is truly an honor to meet such an illustrious general."

"The Emperor has been such a wise person to talk to," said Jenny. "He is so very charming, full of wit and wisdom."

"Ah," I said, "perhaps the general can give me some military advice."

"Oui, mon ami, the best advice I can give you is when you make a battle plan, always, but always, have a back-up plan," Napoleon advised, "for I have found that plans often go astray in zee heat of zee battle."

"Thank you, sir; I shall always keep that in mind."

Jenny smiled at me and said, "Colonel, you don't know how relieved I am that you came to my rescue. There is no telling what the Yankees would have done to......"

Just then a rooster crowed. I blinked my eyes open and discovered I was in my bunk. What a strange dream, I know Jenny is not a spy, and Napoleon has been dead for 44 years!

After dressing and making our bunks we fell into formation outside the dormitory. It was dark and foggy that last morning of February. The fog was so thick that you couldn't see more than ten feet in front of you. Like the English say, it was "thick as pea soup."

Cadet Lt. Randolph marched us to the front of the school where we waited patiently for Captain Johnson.

Because of the dense fog the color ceremony was brief. After the national flag was hoisted the captain gave a short speech about how important it was in this time of war shortages to tighten our belts. He said because of the blockade it was getting increasingly difficult to obtain sugar, flour, salt, cloth, coffee, etc.

"I've heard some complaints about the food in the mess hall. Men, please remember, we have to make sacrifices for the cause," explained our Principal.

The captain finished up with, "as usual we will have marching drill at 3 o'clock. Please, don't be late."

We marched to the mess hall for breakfast, and soon after eating I went to my first class of the day, Mr. Frazier's Ancient History class. Mr. Frazier was my favorite teacher. He always made history interesting, and brought our dry history books to life with his enthusiastic lectures about the Greeks and Romans. This morning's lecture was on Julius Caesar's war in Gaul and as usual Mr. Frazier had every student's full attention as he explained how Caesar went about conquering Gaul.

After my history class was finished, I headed to Mr. Sartori's French class. I considered French to be a tough language to learn. The French grammar always gave me fits.

The next class was Reverend DuBose's religion class, with an emphasis on Christian morals and ethics. Our school had close ties with the Presbyterian Church here in Tallahassee.

My last class of the morning was Mr. Melton's chemistry class. With Mr. Melton's long hair, brushy moustache, and his unconventional manner, he often gave the impression of being the mad scientist. Although he was a bit eccentric, all the students loved him anyway.

Today Mr. Melton showed us how to make hydrogen by combining sulfuric acid with zinc in one beaker and collecting the hydrogen in another beaker. Don't ask me how he did it, but somehow Tom Archer caused his beaker of hydrogen to explode! It scared the willies out of everyone in the room! Fortunately, Tom was not injured, except for a small cut on his hand.

After Mr. Melton's chemistry class, Luther, Tom Archer, and I headed over to the mess hall. We sat down to a lunch of chicken and rice, beans and corn bread. Sitting at the table behind me was a group of girls from the Female Department of the school. Tom's sister, Sue, was one of them and she giggled while she gossiped with her girl friends.

"Oh, Cadet Murray," she called, "a friend of mine gave me this note to give to you."

Miss Archer handed me a sheet of paper that was folded over in half. I opened it to find a message written in a fine penmanship.

It read:

Dear Eugene,

It was such a pleasure meeting you at church and I was so happy you had dinner with my family. Wasn't the Whist game we played just wonderful?

I asked Sue Archer to give you this note because I wanted you to know that I will be out of town for a while. My Aunt Flora in Thomasville, Georgia has come down with pneumonia and I've gone to nurse her back to health.

I hope to see you again in church when I return.

Sincerely Yours,
Jenny MacLaren

I was happy to get a note from Jenny, but very disappointed that I would not be able to see her next Sunday. I guess I will just have to have patience and wait for her return.

"Go on without me. I need to talk to my sister," said Tom, as we all finished up our meal.

Luther and I exited the Mess Hall. I was showing him the note when we bumped into Eddie and a couple of his friends. Before I knew what was happening, Eddie grabbed the note out of my hand.

"What have we here, Eugene?" asked Eddie. "It looks like a love letter."

"Hey, that's private, Eddie. Give it back!!!"

Eddie smiled and said, "What are you going to do about it if I don't?"

I wanted to sock Eddie with all my might, but fighting at the Military Institute would bring on a severe punishment for both Eddie and me. I had to swallow my pride and get the note back by the best means possible.

"You know, Eugene, your ears are so big someone should cut them off. Maybe I should volunteer for the job," Eddie said with a smirk.

Lucky for me, while Eddie was taunting me, Luther grabbed the note out of his hand and took off running like a jack rabbit. Eddie gave chase, but Luther was one of our fastest athletes and it didn't take Eddie long to realize he wasn't going to catch that Son of Hermes. He gave up the chase.

At the start of English Literature class Luther returned the note to its rightful owner. I was glad to get it back.

As 3 o'clock rolled around, all the cadets fell into formation out on the parade ground. After a foggy start for the day, the weather had turned out to be pleasant enough. It was a mild but slightly overcast afternoon.

Captain Johnson, looking smart in his frock coat with braided kepi, called the cadets to attention. Just yesterday the seminary received seven Enfield and three Richmond percussion rifled muskets, all .58 calibers. These muskets had been issued to the senior classmen who were very proud to carry modern weapons instead of the obsolete flintlocks like the rest of the cadets.

"Men, before we go into company marching drill, I wish to take a few minutes to show you how to load the new musket in nine times," said the captain.

"Those of you who have been issued the new rifled muskets, please follow my example with your own weapon. Those of you with the flintlocks can follow along as well."

"Number One, Load!"

The boys took their muskets and placed them between their feet, only a few inches from their body, holding the musket with their left hand.

"Number Two, Handle Cartridge!"

With their right hand they went to their cartridge box and retrieved a cartridge.

"Number Three, Tear Cartridge!"

The boys placed the end of the paper cartridge between their teeth and tore it open.

"Number Four, Charge Cartridge!"

They emptied the gunpowder down the barrel, and pulled the bullet from the cartridge, then inserted it into the bore of the musket.

"Number Five, Draw Rammer!"

The boys pulled the rammer out of the pipes. They turned the rammer and placed the head of the rammer on the bullet.

"Number Six, Ram Cartridge!"

They rammed the bullet down the barrel with their rammers.

"Number Seven, Return Rammer!"

The rammers were returned to the musket pipes and with a finger on the head of the rammer forced it home.

"Number Eight, Prime!"

With their left hand the boys raised their muskets to shoulder height, the right hand holding the small of the stock close to their waist. They half cocked their weapon, took a cap out of the cap pouch, placed it on the musket nipple, and then pressed it down with their thumb. The younger boys with flintlocks opened their pan and put a small amount of powder in it and then closed the pan lid.

"Number Nine, Shoulder Arms!"

The cadets brought their muskets to the Shoulder Arms position. They were now ready to fire their weapons.

"We are going to fire a volley," said Johnson.

"Ready!"

Everyone cocked their muskets.

"Prepare to fire at extreme elevation!"

"Aim!"

The cadets aimed their muskets high into the sky.

"Fire!"

KABOOM! Boom! Nearly everyone fired in unison. However, a couple of the younger boys were a bit late.

"We will have to work on our company fire the next time

we are at the firing range. That was a little ragged," the captain commented.

Captain Johnson had us go through the manual of arms, the prescribed drill for carrying the rifle. Then he marched us up and down the parade ground. We practiced going from a column of fours into a line of battle, marching by the flank, and numerous other maneuvers. After over an hour of marching we were all good and tired.

When drill was finished we all went back to our dorm rooms, put our muskets into the racks located at the end of each bunk, and placed our accouterments on pegs located on the wall. We took our cadet jackets off and made ourselves comfortable.

"Hey, thanks for snatching that note out of Eddie's hand, and getting it back to me," I told Luther.

"Don't mention it. What are friends for?" he replied. "By the way, I didn't get to read your note. Can I see it?"

"Sure. Take a look," I said as I passed him the note.

He read it, and then slowly looked up with a big grin on his face.

"I think she likes you."

"Yes, I hope so. Since meeting her I can't think of hardly anything else. Do you believe in 'love at first sight'?" I asked him.

"Heck, I don't know," Luther said with a shrug.

Luther and I talked about Jenny for the rest of the evening, and before I went to sleep I said a little prayer for her safe return.

Chapter 6

On the morning of February 28th the three transports dropped anchor about thirteen miles south of Lighthouse Point. Visibility was limited due to a thick fog, but by noon the fog began to lift. During the afternoon a dozen ships from the blockading squadron joined the transports.

Among the warships was the U.S.S. Moluska, commanded by Captain Gifford. He commanded the blockading fleet, and General Newton took a small boat over to the Moluska to confer with him on the plan of attack.

For the next three hours the two officers discussed the various options available to them. General Newton had brought with him over 900 troops, and the Navy had about half that number sailors. They needed to use these men to best advantage.

In the middle of the meeting Captain Chatfield arrived aboard the Moluska. He had been responsible for the transports successfully reaching their anchorage here so General Newton and Captain Gifford were both pleased to see him.

"Captain Gifford, I must apologize for not patrolling my usual section of the coast. However, while the Magnolia was docked at Key West General Newton requested my services," Chatfield explained.

"I understand, and that is not a problem," said Gifford. "Now, have a seat and join our little conference. We may need your expert knowledge of Florida's coastal waters for the next couple of days."

Captain Chatfield looked around the cabin and found a chair. He pulled it up next to the table where the general and Captain Gifford were sitting. A nautical chart was spread out on the table where General Newton was pointing at a small river a few miles northeast of the lighthouse.

"Gentlemen, the first thing we need to do to shut down the port of St. Marks is to capture the East River Bridge, which I've been told is located about 4 miles northeast of the lighthouse. To that purpose, I wish to have a dozen sailors, under cover of darkness, sneak up to within sight of the bridge, and keep watch to prevent its destruction. While the blue jackets are watching the bridge, Major Weeks' dismounted cavalry will land at the lighthouse, march with all haste to the bridge and capture it," said General Newton.

The general continued, "After we have secured the bridge we will begin landing both the 2nd Regiment and the 99th Regiment. There is a trail that runs north from the lighthouse to Newport on the St. Marks River. Once we get to Newport we will cross the bridge there. Then we can turn south and capture the port of St. Marks, or we can turn north and capture the bigger prize of Tallahassee. All we have to do is cross two bridges, and victory is ours!"

Captain Gifford took a sip of coffee from his pewter mug and said, "At the same time, I propose that we send some of our ships against Fort Ward, the Confederate fort guarding the entrance to the St. Marks River. We'll have to send in our smaller vessels because of the shallow waters around the fort. And this darn fog will make maneuvering around the shore line very difficult, so I plan on sending my best pilot to guide the ships in for the attack on the fort."

"The fog is not all bad, sir. It conceals our fleet, so the rebels have no idea that we are here," said Chatfield.

"Yes, you're right, of course, captain," said the general. "Captain Gifford and I believe you are the best man to supervise the landing of Major Weeks' troops."

"Thank you, sir. I will do my best," Chatfield was grateful for the vote of confidence.

The three officers continued to plan out strategy. It was finally agreed upon to attack the fort tomorrow, and hold off landing at the lighthouse for one more day.

Three schooners and a steamer were tasked with the job of taking the fort. The fog was so thick that even with a good pilot guiding the ships toward St. Marks, navigating was made extremely difficult. The ships glided through the coastal waters like phantoms in the mist. Their ghostly shadows were barely visible to each ship's helmsman.

The small fleet continued on a north by northwest heading, the lead ship making small adjustments guided by its pilot, with the other ships following closely behind.

Then a great calamity occurred. Suddenly, the lead ship ran aground, and before the other ships could alter course they were all stuck on the sand bar as well. Worse yet, it was high tide. They would be stuck there for some time.

"Joe, I don't know 'bout you, but I'm getting tired of being cooped up on this here wooden tub they call a boat. When are we going to land?" complained Joshua.

"I don't know, but I ain't too happy at being at sea, and the first thing I want to do when I get back on land is kiss the good earth," said Joe.

The men on the U.S.S. Honduras were getting tired of the long wait. Except for the short time on Depot Key, they had been onboard ship for days and were eager to be back on solid ground again.

Joshua saw Captain Tracy walking the deck and approached him. He saluted his company commander and asked, "Sir, any word on when we will be landing?"

"Well, Private Jackson, the delay has to do with several of our ships running aground. I'm sure it won't be much longer before we get our orders. Just be patient," advised Tracy.

Later that afternoon a launch pulled up to the Honduras. General Newton had issued orders and soon afterward Captain Tracy called his men together for a briefing.

"Men, I have just received some good news. First thing tomorrow morning Major Weeks' U.S. 2nd Florida Cavalry will capture the East River Bridge. Soon afterward the 2nd US Colored Infantry Regiment will be landed, and will proceed north to Newport, capture the bridge there, and march west to the St. Marks Railroad. Once on the railroad, we will follow it north all the way to Tallahassee, capturing the state capital."

The men gave a loud cheer.

"First Sergeant Fisher, I want you to check and make sure each man in the company is carrying 60 rounds of ammo, two days worth of rations in their haversacks, and a full canteen of water."

"Yes, sir!" Fisher gave an enthusiastic reply. With any luck B Company will be back on dry land very soon.

At twilight, with the cloak of darkness quickly coming on, a dozen hand picked sailors rowed around Lighthouse Point and up the East River. About three miles up the river they put in to shore and pulled their boat up onto the bank. They were about one mile south of the bridge and advanced cautiously, making sure not to make any noises as they felt their way through the marsh. They soon found the trail that led from the lighthouse to the East River Bridge. Creeping slowly, silently up the trail, they were afraid of coming upon a rebel picket. But, luck was with them, there was not a soul to be seen on this side of the bridge.

As soon as they spotted the bridge they took cover in the palmetto bushes. Some moonlight filtered through the pine trees so it wasn't totally dark. Then they saw it, a campfire on the other side of the river. There were Confederate soldiers guarding the bridge after all.

The Union sailors settled in for a long night of watching the bridge. Their job was to make sure the rebs didn't burn it. They were under strict orders not to make any noise, and not to fire at the enemy unless the rebs began to set the bridge on fire. Later the naval unit would be reinforced by Major Weeks' detachment of cavalry and Weeks' men would be responsible for taking the bridge.

The night was quiet, and a light fog began to roll in. The only sounds to be heard were the chirps of the crickets, the croaks of a couple of bull frogs, and an occasional laugh from the camp on the other side of the river.

Long hours passed with no more sounds heard from the enemy camp. It was in the wee hours of the morning when one of the seamen, a fellow by the name of Bill Owens, moved to the edge of a marshy hollow to relieve his bladder. Suddenly, a cottonmouth water moccasin struck him on the side of his calf. He wanted to cry out in pain, but realized that would alert the Confederates. He had left his carbine leaning against a tree, so he pulled out his cutlass and in three quick strokes hacked the serpent into pieces.

Owens made his way over to where the unit leader, Ensign Whitney, was hiding.

"What's wrong?" whispered the ensign.

"I've been snake bit," groaned Owens.

"Where?" asked Whitney.

Owens pointed to a spot on his trouser leg, and Ensign Whitney pulled out his knife. Whitney slit the leg of the breeches up to the knee. There was just enough moonlight for him to see the two puncture marks left by the viper. He cut across the two puncture wounds and began to suck out the poison, spitting each mouthful of the foul tasting stuff onto the ground. Whitney was very careful not to swallow any of the poison.

"Under the circumstances, you are going to have to lay down here and wait for help to arrive with Weeks' men. They should be here before dawn," said Ensign Whitney.

"Ensign, can you give me anything for the pain?" asked Owens.

"All I have is a small flask of rum. Here, take a couple of swigs from this."

Owens drained the small flask, and then settled down to wait out the night.

Time passed slowly.

Whitney kept looking southwest toward the lighthouse. Where are Weeks' men? If they don't get here soon it will be dawn and surely the rebels will discover his sailors.

With the men sitting in the palmetto bushes, in the dark for so many hours, it seemed like the passage of time had come to a stand still. Then, very gradually, the sky began to lighten. Where were their reinforcements?

The ensign saw four men begin to walk across the bridge. So far, they hadn't observed anything out of the ordinary. They don't know they have company, but how long will that last?

The four rebels kept coming. It wouldn't be long before the Union sailors were discovered, and Ensign Whitney needed to do something quick.

Everyone in Whitney's detail had a loaded gun, and was anxiously waiting for his signal.

"Ready!" he shouted.

"Fire!"

The volley shocked and surprised the four pickets. They turned and ran back across the bridge, one limping badly, and another holding his left arm as he ran.

Moments later shots rang out from the other side of the river. From the number of shots, Whitney estimated that there must be at least forty rebels firing at his men. He gave the order to "fire at will".

Both sides keep up a steady rate of fire. Luckily, his men were using the pine trees for cover and so far none of his men had been hit. But, it didn't look good for the sailors. They were outnumbered by at least four to one. On top of that, the Confederates could be seen loading a field cannon. Moments later the gun belched forth a cloud of smoke and two branches were blasted from the side of a nearby tree. Fortunately, the shot had been a little too high.

Then Whitney heard three revolver shots from behind his position. That was the signal to retreat. Finally, Major Weeks' cavalry unit of two hundred dismounted men had arrived.

With the arrival of two hundred rifles, the firefight really heated up. Now the tables were turned, with the Union force vastly outnumbering the rebels.

Accompanying Major Weeks was Captain Chatfield.

"Ensign Whitney, you can take your men back to the ship," ordered Chatfield.

"But, sir, we would like to stay and be a part of the fight," begged Whitney.

"Listen, we need every one of our sailors to man the ships. One sailor is worth a dozen soldiers! So, get your men back to their boat and return to the ship."

"Aye, aye, sir!"

The sailors loaded Owens on to a makeshift stretcher and began to carry him back to the boat. It had been a long night, but they left with a feeling of satisfaction in a job well done since they knew that the bridge would soon be captured.

Captain Chatfield should have gone back with the naval detail, but he decided to stay and watch the fight.

"Major Weeks, my part in this operation has been completed, so I no longer have any authority over you. You are now the commanding officer here," said Chatfield.

The major laughed, "That's fine with me."

"Captain, you might want to keep moving around. If you stand still for too long a sharpshooter will get a bead on you. Your officer's uniform makes you a prime target," commented Weeks.

While Chatfield considered what the major had just said, a bullet shot his officer's shoulder board right off.

"Damn! That was close!" exclaimed the captain.

Chatfield ducked behind a pine tree for cover.

The firefight continued without either side making a move. The Confederate cannon fired a second time, but once again missed hitting anyone.

On Saturday, March 4th, Joshua woke and made his way up to the deck. For the first time in several days there wasn't fog to conceal the seascape. As a bright sun began to rise on the horizon, Joshua could see a dozen ships resting at anchor.

Far to the north he could hear gunshots, and realized that a battle was in progress. Up on the quarterdeck he saw a signalman waving his flags, apparently sending a message to the general's ship, which was near by.

Moments later, Captain Tracy shouted down the hold of the ship, "This is it men! General Newton wants the 2nd Regiment to disembark as soon as possible. Grab your gear and form a line over there by Sgt. Fisher."

Every available boat was transporting men to the shore, and in a short time all of Company B was formed up on the shore within sight of the lighthouse. Captain Tracy ordered his troops to march with all haste toward the bridge, about an hour march away.

When the 2nd Regiment reached the fight around the bridge, Colonel Townsend quickly conferred with Major Weeks. The colonel took in the situation and quickly made a decision.

"Major, the rebels may have reinforcements on the way. Therefore, I am going to charge across that bridge before they have time to set up a strong defense," explained the colonel. "My boys can take it!"

"Fix bayonets!"

"Forward, at the double-quick!"

"March!"

The U.S. 2nd Regiment of Colored Infantry streamed across the bridge. At first the rebels fired at the approaching troops, but by the time the Union troops were half way across, the rebs turned heal and fled into the woods. Two or three men in Company A were wounded during the charge. Otherwise the 2nd Regiment had received light casualties, and not only captured the bridge but also the Confederate cannon as well.

"Splendid! The general will be happy to hear that we took the first of the two bridges. And as soon as the navy brings up the two field cannons, we can continue up to the Newport Bridge and take that as well," said Colonel Townsend.

Later that day General Newton arrived with the rest of the Union force, including two field cannons. With the captured rebel cannon, Newton's force now had three cannons in support of his infantry. The general felt confident that things were going well and before long he would be entering Tallahassee as its conqueror. A promotion would surely follow.

The general decided that since it was late in the afternoon and the Newport Bridge was still five or six miles away, he would have his men camp for the night right here by the East River Bridge and proceed first thing the next morning.

At the crack of dawn, on Sunday morning, the 5th of March, a bugler began to play reveille. Joshua and Joe came out of their dog tent, a tent made by putting two shelter-halves together. Each soldier carried one shelter-half in his knapsack and when attached together the two halves offered just enough room for two men, although many soldiers joked that the tent was only big enough for two dogs, thus the name!

After a quick breakfast of hardtack and coffee the regiment formed up and marched north toward the Newport Bridge. It was a fine morning, and as the troops marched along they could hear mockingbirds singing, and they watched as high in the sky two hawks glided gracefully in the wind.

Because of the three cannons being pulled along the dirt road, the Union force had to keep to a slow pace. It was late morning before they came into sight of the St. Marks River and the bridge at Newport.

"Dang! Can you believe it! They burned the bridge! Now, what are we going to do?" asked Joshua.

"I ain't got a clue," replied Joe.

General Newton stared at the still smoking ruins of the bridge. Now, what was he suppose to do? There didn't appear to be any place in the river that was fordable, so he decided to call a council of war, maybe his senior officers could come up with a good idea.

As luck would have it, some important information was coming his way via Colonel Townsend.

"Sir, one of the local slaves tells me that there is a natural land bridge across the river just seven or eight miles north of here," the colonel proudly stated.

"Excellent! This is, indeed, good news!" exclaimed the general.

"There is just one thing, sir. There is no road going up the east side of the river, just an old Indian trail through the swamp."

"Not to worry, colonel. We can manage."

The soldiers on the other side of the river were taking pot shots at the Union force, and a skirmish platoon from the 99th was returning the fire.

"Colonel, who are those troops that oppose us?" asked the general.

"I believe they are the 5th Florida Cavalry Regiment, led by Col. George Scott, a very capable officer," Townsend replied.

"Yes, I've heard of him," said Newton. "Now, here is my plan. First, I want Major Weeks and his refugee cavalry to stay here. He is to keep firing at Scott's men to hold them here while our main force marches north to this natural bridge. Major Weeks will be responsible for guarding our rear, as well."

"Do you have any questions, major?"

"No, sir," replied Weeks.

"That's fine. Next, as soon as it gets dark we are headed straight for that natural bridge. I want to get there before the rebels do," the general explained.

Sporadic rifle fire continued between the two opposing forces all afternoon. The rebels were reinforced by what looked like some rather young soldiers.

"Joe, did you see those reinforcements?" asked Joshua.

"Well, they ain't real close, but from what I can see, they don't look like no regular army troops," Joe said.

"Oh, yeah, them rebel soldiers getting younger all the time!"

73

Sgt Fisher walked over to where Joshua was standing.

"It will be dark soon and Captain Tracy says to be ready to move out on a moment's notice," Fisher told the men.

As darkness descended on the Florida wilderness, Major Weeks' Union Cavalry took over the job of keeping the Confederates occupied at Newport while the rest of the Union force quietly moved north.

Chapter 7

*I*t was nearly time for "lights out" on this Saturday night. I had just finished rereading the letter from Jenny for the one hundredth time. Since Luther was already up in his bunk, ready to get some shut eye, I stepped over to the table and was about to blow out the candle. Suddenly a shrill whistle could be heard coming from the train station.

What in the world I thought?

It was common knowledge that the two steam locomotives operated between St. Marks and Tallahassee only during the day. It had been dark for more than two hours, so it was very unusual for the train to arrive at this time. And, on top of that, the whistle kept blowing.

"Gene, what in tarnation is all that noise about?" asked Luther.

"I don't know, but it must be something really big. Something important is going on, I'm sure."

"Well, if it's so important, why don't you put on your boots, go outside, and see what all the commotion is about?" suggested Luther.

"Oh, sure, I'm going to run outside in just my night-shirt and boots to see what's happening. No, thanks," I said. "It can wait until morning."

I blew out the candle and crawled into my bunk. Then I pulled my blanket over my head to muffle the train's noise and fell fast asleep.

A railroad was built between the port of St. Marks and Tallahassee in 1837. In those early years of operation, the cars were pulled by mules. But, in 1856 a whole new and improved track was laid and two brand new steam engines were purchased. By the autumn of 1856 the new steam powered train was pulling eight or nine freight cars and one passenger car on a regular basis between the two towns.

On the morning of Saturday, March 4th, Colonel Scott's men were surprised by a small Union force attempting to take the East River Bridge. Or, at least it seemed like a small force at first. However, about an hour and a half later what had looked like a raiding party now turned into a full fledged invasion with a regiment of colored infantry charging across the bridge and capturing it.

After the lost of the bridge at East River, Colonel Scott's troops fell back to the Newport Bridge, some 5 miles away.

Scott realized the importance of this bridge. He decided that it must not fall into enemy hands.

"Men, we must prevent this bridge from being captured. I want every man to search the dock and find anything that will burn, such as tar and pitch, kerosene, turpentine, or whale oil, and start dumping it on the bridge. I want this thing on fire within a quarter hour!" shouted Scott.

While Col. Scott watched the bridge being torched, he composed a message to alert the Governor of the existing danger. He gave the message to one of his trusted men, Billy Denham, and instructed him to ride to St. Marks, take the train into Tallahassee, and to warn the state government.

Bill Denham was a former student of West Florida Seminary. Early in the war he had joined the 1st Florida Infantry Regiment. In his first battle he was wounded and captured. Later he was paroled, and after a period of rest, he recovered from his wounds. As soon as he was fit enough to ride a horse he volunteered for the 5th Florida Cavalry.

Now, Billy hopped onto his beautiful palomino, Hector, a golden horse with white mane and tail, and trotted off to St. Marks to deliver the vital message. When he got to St. Marks, he headed for the train station. He was disappointed to find no sign of the train there.

"I'm sorry, but the train left an hour ago," the ticket agent said.

"Darn! When is the next train?" asked Billy.

"Well, that would be the three-thirty to Tallahassee."

"You mean I have to wait for an hour and a half?" he asked in disbelief.

Billy thought to himself that he should have simply ridden his horse to Tallahassee in the first place. But he was just following orders.

"Look, I have an urgent message I have to get to the Governor. The Yankees have landed at the lighthouse and are trying to cross the St. Marks River," explained Billy.

The ticket agent just looked at Billy. Was the soldier crazy, or a bit drunk? No, he looked normal enough.

"When the train comes in, can we get it to head right back to Tallahassee?" asked Billy.

"No, sir, we stick to a strict schedule. Besides, I heard that a schooner slipped through the blockade and docked here about a half hour ago. I hear it came in with supplies from Cuba, and we have to transfer the cargo from the boat to the train before the train can head back to the capital."

"I see," said Billy. He thought for a moment then added, "Can you tell me where I can water and feed my horse?"

"There's a stable down the street and on the right," the ticket agent said while pointing in that direction.

Billy had some time to wait before the next train would leave the station, so he walked Hector over to the stable, watered and fed his trusty steed, and then he groomed the palomino.

Before long the train pulled into the station. Half a dozen people got off. Stevedores began to unload bales of cotton from the train. They loaded the cotton bales into wagons which were driven to the warehouse for the cotton to be stored until a blockade runner could take the shipment out of port.

Meanwhile, other stevedores were loading the train with the cargo from the schooner that had arrived this afternoon. By quarter past three o'clock the train was loaded and most of the passengers were on board.

Billy purchased tickets for both Hector and himself. A stevedore put the horse in the livestock car while Billy climbed onboard the passenger car.

He settled into his seat and waited for the train to get underway. This trip was not going very smoothly, he thought to himself. He pulled out his pocket watch and checked the time. It was almost three-thirty. He wondered what action he was missing back at the Newport Bridge.

Then he could hear the engine building up steam, and slowly the train began to move. At first the train moved so slow that a person could walk beside it and keep up, but as it left the port town and steamed through the pine forest of Wakulla County, it picked up speed. The trip to Tallahassee would take only about two hours, with a short stop at Woodville, and then another short stop at Bel Air, before arriving at the Tallahassee train station around five-thirty.

The train pulled into Woodville station right on time. After taking on some water for the engine, and gaining a couple of passengers, the train continued on. The engineer had just got the train up to cruising speed when he realized there was something blocking the track up ahead. He began braking right away, and as he got closer he could see that a giant pine tree had fallen across the track. He brought the train to a halt with only five feet to spare between his cow-guard and the tree trunk.

79

Billy was surprised when the train began to brake hard after leaving Woodville. He poked his head out of the window to see what the matter was and discovered a huge pine tree lying across the track.

The engineer came back to the passenger car and climbed on. He gave a long, hard look at the eight passengers. There was an elderly couple, a family of four, a middle aged businessman, and Bill Denham.

"A tree has fallen across the track and I need volunteers to help cut it up and move it out of the way," said the engineer.

Bill and the family man volunteered for the job. They took turns cutting the tree with the one axe that the train carried. As the sun set on the western horizon, Bill could see that the train wouldn't get into town until late. He was trying his best to get the message to Tallahassee, but was meeting one obstacle after another. Oh, the frustration! Thinking about this made him swing that axe just a little harder.

Finally, when both men were on the edge of utter exhaustion, they succeeded in chopping through two places in the trunk. With the help of the engineer and the middle aged businessman, the four men were able to push the tree trunk off the track.

Hallelujah! The train was on its way again!

It was 9 o'clock at night when the locomotive pulled into Tallahassee. Billy had asked the engineer to blow his whistle to help alert the capital to imminent danger.

Billy had his horse off-loaded from the train as quickly as possible. He felt like a modern day Paul Revere when he

80

mounted his horse and galloped to the Governor's Mansion with the important message.

Upon reading the note from Colonel Scott, Governor Milton sent out a telegraph message west to Quincy and east to Lake City requesting help to defend the capital.

The headquarters for the Florida Military District was located in Lake City. Since 1864 General William Miller had been in command. He was an experienced combat leader who, early in the war, had commanded the First and Third Florida Infantry Regiments, that is, until he was wounded at Murfreesboro, Tennessee.

At 10 o'clock on that Saturday night General Miller was awakened from his slumbers by a pounding on his front door. The general came down the stairs in his night-shirt carrying a kerosene lantern for light. Standing at his front door was a staff officer holding a telegram.

"Come in, major," said Miller.

"Thank you. Sir, this is an important message from the governor." The major handed General Miller the note.

"Good God! The Yankees have landed at St. Marks and are marching on Tallahassee! And the governor wants me to take over the field command!"

Miller wrote a quick note and handed it to the major. The note told Colonel J. Daniels to have his troops ready to go when the train arrived in Madison on Sunday.

"Please take this message to the telegraph office and send it to Colonel J. Daniels, commanding the First Regiment of Reserves in Madison."

"Yes, sir," the major said as he left in haste.

At 6 o'clock on Sunday morning Cadet Lt. Byrd Coles came running into the dormitory shouting for everyone to wake up. I wasn't sure what he was saying, but it had something to do with the Yankees landing at St. Marks. Coles told us that Captain Johnson wanted everyone to fall into formation in just twenty minutes.

"Now, we know what all that commotion was about last night," I commented, as I quickly put on my uniform and tied my brogans, the low cut infantry boot.

Minutes later I was standing in formation. As soon as we were all in the ranks, Captain Johnson began to address us.

"Cadet Corps! I have some important news to tell you. A force of over fourteen hundred Yankees has landed at St. Marks and is marching on Tallahassee at this very moment!"

A murmur went through the ranks.

"The governor has called out the militia and has requested our help as well," explained the captain. "Men, just as the brave cadets of the Virginia Military Institute last May fought in the Battle of New Market, this is our opportunity to serve our country with honor and glory!"

The boys gave a cheer.

"Once we get all of our muskets and accoutrements together, we will march to the State Capitol Building and be

sworn into the Confederate Army. I want you to understand just how dangerous this job could be. Now, please
raise your hand if you wish to volunteer."

Every single boy raised his hand.

"Excellent! However, I want every boy who has family
living here in Tallahassee to go home and bring me back a
note giving parental permission to be a part of this," said
Johnson. "And get back here as quick as you can!"

"The rest of you can march over to the mess hall and
get some breakfast. I want everyone back here, armed and
ready to go, no later than 11 o'clock."

"Formation is dismissed!"

While Luther and I marched to the mess hall with the
rest of the cadets from out of town, the local cadets quickly
headed home to plead with their parents for permission to
join the fight.

After breakfast I wrote a one page letter to my folks.
I told my mother how much I loved her and, if she was
reading this letter, I had died for God and country. I put
the letter in an envelope and wrote "To Mr. and Mrs. Wm.
Murray" on the front, and then placed it on my table. My
parents would get this letter should anything happen to me
in the coming battle.

Luther liked my idea of writing the letter and before I
had finished my first paragraph he was starting a letter of
his own.

As 11 o'clock rolled around, all the cadets began to as-
semble on the parade ground. Everybody was excited. We
were a little scared, yet we all looked upon this as a great
adventure.

Roll was called to make sure everyone had made it back alright, and Captain Johnson was pleased to see that all the local lads had brought back the permission notes, as requested.

We formed up and marched up the hill to the Capitol where Governor Milton was waiting for us. The news of the invasion had stirred up things on this Sunday morning, and a small crowd was gathered in front of the Capitol Building. Among those gathered were six or seven teenage boys with muskets who begged with Captain Johnson to be included in his Cadet Company. The captain spoke with the young men and after he was satisfied that they would fit into his ranks without a problem, gave his approval for them to join. He told them to fall in at the rear of the company.

Governor Milton gave a patriotic speech, telling us that we are fighting for our homes, and that with God's help we would stop the invader. We were all moved by the man's words.

"Three cheers for Governor Milton!" shouted Captain Johnson.

The boys gave a hearty cheer.

"Hip Hip Hurray!"

"Hip Hip Hurray!"

"Hip Hip Hurray!"

Then the governor swore us all into the Confederate Army.

We marched down Monroe Street with our fife and drummer playing Dixie and the Bonnie Blue Flag. Then we turned at Gaines Street and were pleased to see people lining the street waving to us as we passed by. Continuing on we soon arrived at the railroad station. A throng of people were waiting for us there, including all the girls from the Female Department of the Seminary. I recognized Susan Archer, Tom's sister, waving her handkerchief at us as we came to a halt. She gave me a sweet smile.

It was while we waited for the train that Captain Johnson told the youngest cadets that they could not go with us. One of the "Baby Cadets" began to cry.

"It just ain't fair, sir!" the young boy said between sobs.

"Son, you're the only child of a mother who is blind. I can not permit the possibility of you becoming a casualty of war. Your poor mother needs you. I'm sorry but you must stay behind," explained Johnson.

"Professor Sartori, please take these young boys back to the campus."

I watched the Modern Languages teacher gather up our youngest cadets and start the short walk back to the seminary. The group walked back in a very gloomy manner, with their heads hanging down, and with a sullen, dismal look about them. It was sad that they couldn't be a part of this grand adventure, yet I agreed with our Principal's decision not to allow the youngest boys to participate in what could be a bloody battle.

Susan Archer ran over to her brother, Tom, and gave him a hug.

"Brother, you take care of yourself now, you hear?" she said.

Then she did something completely unexpected. She came over to Luther and gave him a kiss on the cheek. He turned bright red with embarrassment. So, it wasn't me she had been smiling at earlier, but rather Luther! I would never have guessed.

"Hey, I see the train coming!" shouted Charles Beard, a 15 year old cadet.

The train blew its whistle and rang its bell as it came to a stop next to the station platform. It was pulling five cars full of various kinds of freight, two empty flatbed cars, and a nearly empty passenger car.

About two dozen of our cadets filed onto the passenger car, and the rest of us had to get onto a flatbed car for the trip south. Luther and I, along with our company's fife player and drummer, had to sit on the flatbed.

Because of the urgency of the matter, the train didn't stop at Bel Air or Woodville but continued down the track. It was after we passed Woodville that a terrible accident occurred. Our drummer boy, Dick Frazer, was fooling around playing with his drum sticks when he dropped one of the sticks. He attempted to catch it, but lost his balance and fell head first over the side of the flat car, breaking his left arm in the fall. The engineer never saw what happened, and the train continued speeding down the track.

The train came to a halt at Wakulla Station, located due west of Newport. The sound of gun fire could be heard in the distance. We jumped down off of the train and began the march to the small port town.

As we approached Newport we could see that most of the bridge had been destroyed, and its ruins continued to smoke. A firefight was in progress between Scott's troops, who were fighting from behind a breastwork they had thrown up, and the Union skirmishers on the other side of the river.

Captain Johnson told us to run two at a time to the Confederate trenches. Luther and I rushed across about 50 yards of open ground to the trench and jumped in. We watched the rest of our company dash to the safety of the trench, but one of our cadets, Sgt. John Dubose, suddenly pitched forward falling face first unto the turf as he made his dash across the exposed ground. As a couple of shots rang out from across the water just before he fell, I was sure he had been shot dead. Two seconds later he picked himself up and finished his run to safety. Fortunately, he had just tripped over a root. Whew, that was a close one; I thought the minister's son had become a casualty.

"Luther, it looks like the Yanks are still thinking about trying to get across what is left of that bridge," I said.

"Yep, but they just ain't brave enough to try it," Luther replied.

Both sides were firing very sparingly, so as not to use up their ammunition. The firing continued until it was totally dark, and then there was a general cease fire.

Shortly after dark, Bill Denham arrived with a message from General Miller. It directed Colonel Scott's 5th Cavalry to move north to defend Natural Bridge from a possible Union attempt to cross there.

Colonel Scott called Captain Johnson over for an officer's meeting.

"I've received orders for my men to ride to Natural Bridge and defend it while reinforcements arrive. General Miller believes the Union will try to cross at that location, so my unit needs to get there first," said Scott.

"What about the cadets?"

"I want your company to hold this position tonight. If I need you at Natural Bridge I will send for you first thing tomorrow morning."

"As you wish, Colonel," said Johnson.

After the 5th Florida Cavalry rode north up the Plank Road things got pretty quiet. Although we could see some campfires on the other side of the river, we had the feeling that the most of the Yanks had pulled out.

I could hear Frank Damon, our youngest cadet with us on that dark night, complaining about being scared. The poor boy would not be twelve years old for a couple of months yet, but he was trying to do a man's job. Some how he had convinced Captain Johnson to allow him to go with us, when all the other ten and eleven year olds had been made to stay behind.

A few feet down the trench from me I could hear Herman Damon talking to Eddie Northrop. Herman, Frank's older brother, was about my age and Frank looked up to him in a big way.

"Herman, why don't you go over to Frankie and talk to him, I think he must be afraid of the dark or something" I said.

"Eugene, why don't you keep your big nose out of Herman's business," retorted Eddie.

"Hey, I was just trying to help," I explained.

"Gene is right, I should go over and calm him down a bit," said Herman.

While Herman was talking to Frank to sooth his fears, Eddie came over to where Luther and I were kneeling.

"Did ya'll see those Union soldiers before it got dark?" asked Eddie.

"Yes, what about 'em?" I asked.

"It looked like most of 'em was darkies, to me."

"So, what if they were?" I asked.

"Eugene, I'll bet most of them is runaway slaves. Yep, the Federal government takes our runaway slaves, gives them a blue suit, puts a weapon in their hands, and sends 'em down here to overthrow our government. That just ain't right! And besides that, my pa always says they ain't as smart as us white folk."

"Eddie, they may have been slaves at one time, but they sure as hell look like soldiers to me, and real good ones at that!"

"And another thing, Eddie, I don't believe they are as dumb as you think," I told him.

"That may be, but if I get half a chance I wouldn't hesitate a second to stick one of 'em through the gut with my bayonet," bragged Eddie.

With that parting comment, Eddie went back to his position in the trench. I was glad he was gone.

Our cadet company had two platoons, and each platoon had two squads. Captain Johnson had each squad take a turn at watch during the night. The night went by very peacefully, and at first light on Monday morning, 6th March 1865, a messenger rode up to our captain.

"Sir, Colonel Scott requests that your cadet company march immediately to Natural Bridge," the cavalryman told Johnson.

Within minutes we were marching up the Plank Road. I had a feeling things were about to get pretty hot. A battle was brewing.

Chapter 8

The going was tough that night as the Federal force worked its way up an old trail that was overgrown in many places. It didn't help that they were dragging three cannons through a lush wilderness either.

There was just enough moonlight for Joshua to make out Major Lincoln and Captain Tracy walking together just a little ahead, off to the side of the column. They were just close enough for him to make out what was being said.

"I wasn't an abolitionist before the war, but the experiences I have had in the last three years of this bloody Civil War have totally changed my attitudes toward the Negro and the question of slavery in the United States," Major Benjamin Lincoln said.

Captain Tracy nodded his head and said, "Although I'm from Delaware, I graduated from the College of New Jersey at Princeton. It was while studying there that I became an ardent abolitionist."

"We need to do what we can to help these people become productive, successful members of society, and to bring about an end to a most evil institution," said the major.

"I whole-heartedly agree, sir."

"And, another thing, Edward, I most fully endorse the reading classes you started back at Fort Myers for all the illiterate troops in your company. I know you will agree with me on this point: Reading is the key to knowledge. The first step on the road to success is a good education."

"Indeed it is, sir."

The Union soldiers struggled on. Many curses were heard that night due to low tree limbs, and the constant danger of tripping over roots or stepping into holes in the dark.

Over 175,000 blacks served in the Union Army in the last two years of the Civil War. For both the black soldiers and their white officers prejudice was a constant problem. For example, black enlisted men received $10.00 per month regardless of rank, whereas white privates made $13.00 a month, white corporals $17.00, and white sergeants $21.00 a month.

Another problem due to prejudice was getting the government to issue regiments in the U.S. Colored Troops the same weapons that white troops were getting. A good example of this is what happened to the 2nd US Colored Infantry. In April 1864 an army inspector condemned over 300 smoothbore muskets from this regiment and had them replaced with new Springfield rifled muskets. The regiment was very pleased to get the new weapons, however, when Colonel Townsend requested new Springfield rifles for the other six companies under his command, he was denied his petition. Over the next eleven months the colonel petitioned for new rifles again and again, but nothing came of it. Thus, as the soldiers tramped toward Natural Bridge only Companies A, B and G were carrying the Springfield rifled muskets. All the rest had old smoothbore muskets.

The 2nd US Colored Regiment led the Union column up the east side of the river, with the 99th US Colored Regiment following. Bringing up the rear was the naval detachment that had the three cannons.

"Josh, dis here is hell trying to march through dis swamp!" complained Joe.

"Oh, you always complainin 'bout something," Joshua said. "You complained when we was sittin on the boat. Now, you complainin 'bout takin a little walk through the woods."

"It's a soldier's right to complain, Joshua."

At that very moment, Sam, the soldier right in front of Joshua, pushed a branch out of his way and let go of it.

Thwack!

It hit Joshua right in the mouth, splitting his lip.

"Ouch! Dammit!"

"Hey, you tryin to kill me?" Joshua asked Sam.

"Sorry," Sam mumbled.

"Well, watch it."

Joshua reached inside his sack coat's breast pocket and pulled out his handkerchief. He dabbed the cloth on his lip, wiping away the blood. This was going to take a long time to heal.

B Company continued its march up the St. Marks. After a time it began to slowly get lighter. At last, the men could see where they were going. Looking ahead, Joshua could see General Newton and Colonel Townsend leading the column, just ahead of A Company, 2nd USCT.

Joshua heard Colonel Townsend tell the A Company commander to send out skirmishers.

"Skirmishers out!" commanded the captain. A platoon from A Company spread out ahead of the Union column, shielding its advance.

Not ten minutes had passed when they ran into Confederate pickets. The sound of two musket shots rang out, breaking the silence of the morning, alerting everyone to the presence of enemy soldiers.

General Newton was disappointed to discover that the rebels were guarding the land bridge. He had a quick conference with Colonel Townsend and Major Lincoln. Joshua could see the general pointing in the direction of the river, giving Major Lincoln some instructions.

The major ran back to our company.

"Captain Tracy, have your men ready to move out at my command!" ordered Major Lincoln.

The major ran down the line to where G Company was located and gave them the same order.

"All right, Companies B and G follow me. Forward, march!" the major shouted.

The two Union companies moved out at a brisk step, with Major Lincoln leading the way.

"By company into line of battle, march!"

B Company quickly shifted into a battle line of two ranks. On Joshua's left he could feel Joe's elbow bump into his own as they struggled through a rough terrain of palmettos. Ahead he could see the Confederate pickets falling back as the Union force advanced at a steady pace.

As the enemy pickets retreated, they fired at the advancing soldiers in blue. Since they were firing on the move, their shots were not very accurate. In a matter of minutes, Joshua saw the rebel pickets run across a stretch of ground that bridged the river. He could see that the river flowed underground for about 100 feet then came up again on the other side. This was the gateway to capturing the state capital of Tallahassee, and all they had to do was get their force across it.

As Joshua's company approached the land bridge they came under a strong fire from both rifles and a battery of cannons. This was totally unexpected. They had made a forced march all night, only to find the land bridge was defended. To make matters worse, the Union artillery was still far to the rear.

With his sword drawn and held high, Captain Tracy shouted, "Forward, men!"

The rebel defenders kept up a steady rate of fire, and each time one of their cannons went off a shiver went up Joshua's spine. The thundering explosion of the cannons was so intimidating that, for just a second, Joshua thought about turning and running. But no, he couldn't let Joe and all his other buddies down. So, he said a little prayer asking for heavenly protection and marched on.

The battle line had just reached the land bridge when a rebel cannon, likely a 12 pounder "Napoleon", fired canister. The shot tore through the center of G Company. A half dozen or more men went down screaming. The rest of the men in G Company panicked at the sight of so many wounded at one time. They turned and ran for cover.

Major Lincoln immediately ordered a general retreat. Joshua and the rest of B Company fell back in an orderly fashion. The two companies retreated for about three hundred yards back into the pine woods. At that point Major Lincoln ordered a halt.

"Companies B and G, I want you to dig rifle pits right here, and also here," the major pointed to a sandy area that was covered by fallen pine needles.

While the two companies were busy digging rifle pits, Major Lincoln strode back to where General Newton and his staff had been watching the skirmish through binoculars.

"I'm sorry, sir, but the enemy has a very strongly defended position. We need artillery support," explained Lincoln.

"Yes, I concur, we need to wait until our cannons arrive on site. In the mean time, I want your battalion to keep up a skirmish with the rebels. While you are keeping our friends in gray busy, I will send the 99th US Colored Infantry back down the river to find another place to ford," the general said.

General Newton was using the 99th US Colored Regiment as his reserve regiment. The main reason for this was the regiment's past history. Although it was now an infantry regiment, until lately it had been known as the 15th US Colored Engineers. Back in April and May of 1864, they were engaged in the Red River Campaign, building bridges, repairing roads, etc.

The general could have ordered the 99th to build a bridge across the St. Marks, but they simply didn't have the time and materials. In addition, building a bridge under enemy fire would have been hazardous in the extreme. So, they looked for a shallow place to cross the water instead.

After searching for about a mile down the river, they came to a spot that looked fordable. There was just one problem; elements of the 5th Florida Cavalry were guarding it. Once again the Federal forces were frustrated in their attempt to cross the river. They exchanged a few shots with the enemy, and then returned to Natural Bridge.

While the 99th searched down the river for a place to ford, Privates Joshua Jackson and Joe Henry dug out their rifle pit using their bayonets and tin plates because, unlike modern soldiers, they didn't carry a shovel as part of their kit. As they franticly dug down through the sand, they threw it in front of the pit creating a barrier of protection against enemy bullets.

"I wonder how long it will be before the Navy brings up our cannons," said Joshua as he kneeled in the safety of the rifle pit.

"I don't know," replied Joe. "But one thing I do know is dis, if I sees a whipping post anywhere between here and Tallahassee, I going to smash it to a million pieces! And dat ain't no lie!"

"Yeah, I'll help ya," agreed his friend.

"Josh, do me a favor, I ain't too good at spellin' just yet. Can ya write on dis here paper, 'To Tallahassee or Hell', asked Joe?

"I sho' can," said Joshua as he printed it out with a pencil from his haversack.

He handed the strip of paper to Joe who stuck in the front of his forage cap.

"As soon as we get our cannons here, we goin' to take dis here bridge and march all de way to Tallahassee! But if I fall in battle, I fall in defense of my race and country!" said Joe with enthusiasm.

"Amen, brudder!" declared Joshua.

Captain Tracy ordered his men to fire at will, but only at definite targets. He warned them not to waste ammunition as this could turn into a long fight. And so, as the morning hours slowly passed by, the 2nd US Colored Infantry continued to skirmish with the defenders of the land bridge while they waited for artillery support.

Chapter 9

"I wish we still had a drummer. It always makes marching easier," Luther said.

"Yeah, it's easier to stay in step. Too bad about Dick," I said. "What a shame he had that accident."

It was a comfortable, cool Monday morning as the cadets marched up the Plank Road. Our poor drummer boy had fallen off of the train during the trip to Wakulla Station, severely injuring himself. Everyone liked the boy, and his drum playing was greatly missed.

During our march to the bridge sporadic gun fire could be heard in the distance, from time to time. Then when we had about two miles to go, the sound of full volleys of gun fire erupted. The artillery fire was especially loud.

"It sounds like we're missing out on a full fledged battle," I commented, half wishing to be elsewhere.

"Yeah, I hope it's not over before we get there," said Luther with a smile. "They need to leave us a few Yanks!"

We laughed.

"You're not scared just a little," I asked?

"Gosh, Gene, maybe a little bit. What about you?"

"I know we're supposed to be brave cadets, but I've got to admit, I am a tad bit worried."

The cadets continued their march up the road with Captain Johnson in the lead. Professors Melton and Frazier brought up the rear, making sure that none of the boys fell too far behind. At the end of each twenty minute period of marching Captain Johnson gave his cadet company a five minute rest. This allowed the younger boys a chance to keep up with the rest of the company.

On the west side of the Plank Road, about a mile from the battlefield, stood a cabin with a wooden shingle roof. On the porch stood a woman wearing a white apron, holding the hands of her two small children, watching us march up. Also standing on the porch were two surgeons waiting for the wounded to arrive.

Captain Johnson halted our company in front of the cabin porch. He walked over to one of the doctors and introduced himself.

"Good morning, sir. I'm Captain Valentine Johnson from the West Florida Seminary. Do you require any assistance with your surgery? I could detail two of my cadets to help you."

"That would be most kind of you," replied the doctor with a white goatee. "Mrs. Byrd has graciously opened up her home to be used as a field hospital, but her nursing will be limited due to having to keep an eye on her two small children. So, two of your cadets would be a great help to us at this time. I'm much obliged."

Our most recent recruit was none other than the governor's fourteen year old son, John Milton, Jr., and our captain saw this field hospital as an opportunity to keep the governor's son out of harm's way.

"Privates Tom Archer and John Milton you are hereby assigned duty as orderlies with this field hospital. Fall out!" commanded Johnson.

The two cadets left the column and walked up the steps to the porch.

They leaned their muskets up against the cabin wall and, turning back, looked down the dirt road toward Natural Bridge.

"Look!" shouted Tom Archer. "Here come a couple of stretchers with wounded on them."

The first stretcher was carrying a man with a bloody left shoulder. He was grimacing with pain and blood was dripping from the canvas stretcher.

"Put him on the table," said the younger of the two doctors.

Mrs. Byrd had volunteered her dinner table to be the operating table. Along one side of it was a set of operating instruments. Once the wounded man was in place the doctor began searching for the bullet with his probe.

Meanwhile, the other stretcher bearers came up to the porch and gently laid the man down. He was a Confederate officer, shot in the chest. His lifeless, pale face told the cadets he was dead.

At the sight of the dead man, the younger boys became

frightened. A couple of the boys even began to cry. Captain Johnson could see that at any moment the younger boys might break ranks and run. He needed to do something fast to regain the confidence of the lads.

"Cadets, don't lose heart! Remember, you must uphold the honor of the South! We are desperately needed here to stop the Yankees from taking our hometown. Please, you must be brave and help defend our homes!" encouraged Johnson.

The speech worked a miracle on the young lads. They settled down and regained their composure.

Captain Johnson marched the cadets the rest of the way to the battlefield where he quickly found General Miller.

"Good morning, sir! The West Florida Seminary Cadet Corps, reporting for duty," said the captain with a salute.

"Thank you, Captain Johnson. I believe your cadets can best be used as guards for the Kilcrease Artillery. I want you to position them just to the left of their guns. Oh, and tell your boys not to shoot unless the Federal troops attack their position."

"Yes, sir," replied the captain.

The Confederate breastworks were shaped in a crescent so that all their firepower could be concentrated on the land bridge. It was a very defensible position, as the Union force was about to find out.

Captain Patrick Houstoun's Kilcrease Artillery held the all important center position. His battery was made up of two 12 pounder cannons and two 6 pounders.

Colonel Love's Militia was located to the right of the Kilcrease guns. Defending the southern end of the crescent was the Milton Artillery, with Colonel Daniel's First Florida Reserves from Madison backing them up.

And finally on the northern end of the crescent was the Gadsden Grays, a militia unit from Quincy made up of men between 50 and 65 years of age. They got their militia's name from all the gray hair and beards worn by each and every soldier in the unit.

Captain Johnson double-timed the cadets to their position just to the left of Houstoun's artillery. They immediately began to strengthen the breastworks that the militia had started. About fifty yards behind them was the Confederate commander's command post, where General Miller and his adjutant, Major William Poole, could observe the battle and lead the Rebel defense.

"Cadets, I want you to remember two things during this battle. First, don't expose yourselves unnecessarily. And secondly, don't fire on the enemy unless they attack the battery you are defending," ordered Johnson.

Since the Union attack on the land bridge earlier that morning things had been fairly quiet.

"I wonder what the Yankees are waiting for," I commented.

Cadet Lt. Byrd Coles, who was standing nearby, overheard my comment and said, "Maybe they're waiting for their artillery to arrive."

"Lieutenant, do you have the time?" asked Luther.

Byrd Coles pulled out his pocket watch. "It's eleven o'clock."

"Thanks," said Luther. "I'm getting hungry. When is lunch?"

"You're always hungry!" I chuckled.

Then all hell broke loose.

BOOM! BOOM! BOOM!

Three cannons from across the river opened up on us, but luckily they were aiming too high.

"Dang, Gene, just look at all the bark and branches being shot out of the surrounding trees!" shouted Cadet Lt. Byrd Coles as he kneeled behind me.

"Yeah, it's a sight," I agreed. "Let's hope they keep aiming too high, or we're going to be in big trouble."

I looked over to my right and watched Captain Houstoun's battery loading their four cannons. On the far right side, the Milton Artillery was already loaded and waiting for the signal from General Miller to begin their barrage. The cannon closest to me was a 12 pounder, and I watched the crew finish loading it by ramming the cannonball down the tube with a long wooden rammer.

At a signal from General Miller, the Confederate cannons began to fire one after the other, right down the line.

BOOM! BOOM! BOOM! BOOM! BOOM!

The ground shook with the explosive firings of the cannons. It sounded like rolling thunder, and when the barrage was over the rebel defenders gave a hearty rebel yell.

By the time the smoke had cleared I could just make out a line of dark shapes coming through the woods. There could be no mistaking who they were, for right in the middle of the line I could see the Stars and Stripes waving in the breeze. The Union infantry was attacking in force.

"Here they come!!!" I shouted.

Captain Johnson was talking to Captain Houstoun when he heard my shout of alarm. He rushed over to a central position behind us.

"Cadets! Hold your fire until I give the order," shouted our captain.

The men in blue halted just short of the land bridge. I watched them raise their muskets in unison and about two seconds later they fired a battalion volley. A cloud of gun smoke rolled toward us. Just before they fired I had the good sense to duck my head down. A piece of bark from the pine log I was hiding behind was blown into a hundred splinters flying just over my head. If I hadn't ducked I would now be laying on the ground with a bullet through my skull.

"Whoa! That was far too close for comfort!" I exclaimed.

"Did anyone get hit?" asked Professor Melton from behind a large pine tree just to our rear. Lucky for us all the bullets just fired were too high, so none of the cadets were hit.

"No, sir," came back the reply.

"For God's sake, keep your heads down!" shouted Professor Melton.

I took a quick peak over the breastworks to see what was going on. The enemy started to advance. I could see that they were coming on three battle lines deep. As they marched across the land bridge the militia companies to our right and left opened up on them.

In another minute or so they would be right up to the Kilcrease Artillery's guns. I looked back at Captain Johnson in anticipation.

"Cadets!" Johnson shouted. "Fire by company!"

"Ready!"

"Aim!"

Every cadet took aim at the oncoming Federals. I held the butt of my Enfield tightly against my shoulder and aimed right at the center of the Union line.

"Fire!" shouted Captain Johnson.

I pulled the trigger and KABLAM!

The captain ordered, "Fire at will!"

The Federal line was still advancing, and I was loading my musket as fast as I could. Would the enemy overrun our position? I'm afraid I would find out the answer to that question in less than thirty seconds!!!

But then, all four of the Kilcrease cannons fired at the same time. They fired canister right into the center of the Federal battle line. BOOM!

Dozens of Union soldiers were cut down in that full battery firing. Large gaping holes could be seen in the enemy lines, and the cries of their wounded were very disturbing. The firing of all those cannons at the same time broke the spirit of the enemy attack. They began to fall back across the land bridge, taking their wounded with them.

"Cease fire!" ordered Captain Johnson.

After the Union retreated from the field I took a good look at the battlefield and could see five bodies laying perfectly still in the middle of the land bridge. It was strange to think that just a few minutes ago those five men were full of hope for a new tomorrow. Yet now they lie lifeless far from their homes, on the banks of this Florida river.

"Gene, I reckon the Yankees have gone off to lick their wounds," said Luther. "Gosh, I'm so hungry right now, I could eat a horse!"

Before the cadets left the seminary yesterday they were each issued two biscuits, a large slice of corn bread, and three cooked sausage links. They carried these food rations in their haversacks.

"Yeah, me too," I said. "I ate most of my rations last night. What do you have left?"

"Gee, all I've got are these pieces of crumbled up corn bread," lamented Luther.

"Hey, too bad, I still have a biscuit and a sausage link!" I bragged. "You should have eaten the corn bread first, my friend, while it was still in one piece."

We had skipped our breakfast that morning because of the summons to reinforce Natural Bridge and trying to eat on the march was just too much bother. Now, we wolfed down what rations we still had left and washed it down with water from our canteens.

I had a feeling the Yanks weren't done with us yet.

Chapter 10

"*L*ook, Joe, I see Colonel Pearsall returning with de 99th, and he don't look too happy," Joshua said.

Lieutenant Colonel Uri Pearsall, commanding the U.S. 99th Colored Infantry, had hoped to find another way across that blasted river, but to no avail. He returned with the bad news that the only way to get across the river was right here, and that was something General Newton would not want to hear.

"At least de Navy is finally here with de big guns," said Joe.

It was late morning before the naval artillery caught up with the infantry. The sight of the Navy dragging its cannons into position was nothing but pure joy to General Newton. Now, at last, he could take that blasted land bridge and get on with capturing the state capital.

The general issued orders for the attack to begin. He

would begin with his artillery and after a brief barrage he would send in his best regiment, the U.S. 2nd Colored Infantry. Colonel Townsend would be in command of the right wing of the attack and Major Lincoln would have the left wing.

Normally companies A and B would be on the far right of the regimental battle line, but General Newton wanted his best armed companies to attack across the land bridge under Major Lincoln's leadership, so he moved them over to the left wing of the regiment. As for the right wing of the attack, the general was hoping that Colonel Townsend's troops would find a way across the river and outflank the enemy.

While the Union cannons fired round after round at the enemy in preparation for the infantry attack, the soldiers in Company B made ready for the job ahead of them.

Captain Tracy looked up and down his company's line, and addressed his men. "Boys, I'm afraid to say this, but by the end of the day you will either be victorious or returned to slavery."

Joe gave Joshua a worried look.

"Captain, you need not fear, I will gladly lay down my life for Liberty!" shouted Joshua.

"Me too, sir!" shouted several others.

"Thank you. I know you all are brave men and will do your duty," said Tracy. "Good luck and God bless."

Joshua was standing in the front rank with Corporal Andy Bates on his right side and Joe Henry on his left. Directly behind him was standing tall, slim Sam Clark from Alexandria, Virginia. Sgt. John Fisher, big nosed and wearing spectacles, was standing a few paces behind them all as a file closer. Everyone was anxious to get started.

"Battalion, forward, march!" shouted Major Benjamin Lincoln.

The four companies that made up the left wing began to advance at a steady pace. In order to get across the narrow land bridge the major "stacked" his companies, first Company A, then Company B, and finally Companies G & H in the last battle line.

The color guard, six paces ahead of the line, was leading the battalion straight for the Natural Bridge. The standard bearer, Sgt. Charlie Hill, carried the national banner with pride. He was accompanied by five corporals acting as honor guards.

When the left wing arrived at the land bridge, the soldiers were ordered to halt.

"Company A, kneel!"

Everyone in the first company took a knee, including the color guard.

"Companies A and B, prepare to fire by battalion!" shouted Major Lincoln.

"Ready"

"Aim"

"Fire!"

Blaam! A huge cloud of smoke rolled toward the rebels.

"Company A, rise!"

"Battalion, forward, march!"

The rebel militia began to shoot at the Union force. Bullets were buzzing by Joshua's head like bees gone mad.

"Joe, dis here kitchen is gettin' mighty hot!" exclaimed Joshua.

The soldier just to Joe's left threw up his hands and screamed as blood squirted out the side of his neck onto Joe's cheek and collar. The soldier fell forward while grabbing his throat. As the line continued forward, Joshua could still hear the dying man's death gurgle.

Joshua glanced to his right and could see some of Colonel Townsend's right wing troops attempting to cross the river. It was simply too deep for the soldiers to wade across. The next time he looked over that way he saw them climbing back up the riverbank. They would just have to be content with firing at the rebel defenders from the east side of the river.

The narrowest part of the land bridge was only about one hundred feet wide. This acted like a bottle neck. Even though each of the 2nd Regiment's companies only averaged about 70 men, due to illness and casualties, Company B was hard pressed to squeeze even this small number through the narrow gap.

From his position behind Company A, Joshua watched the company ahead of him bend like a bow to squeeze through the narrowest part. Then it was his company's turn and Joshua felt the men on his sides press hard against his shoulders. He was beginning to have a hard time breathing because of the crush.

On the far left of the line Joshua heard Cpl. Williams yell, "Give right!" The men on that end of the line were up to their knees in water.

Then they were through.

Joshua looked ahead and could see breastworks about

ninety yards ahead and up a gentle rise. The quicker they covered that distance the better, he thought to himself. He didn't like the look of those four cannons staring straight at him. It was like looking into the Jaws of Death.

Everyone picked up the pace. Now there were just forty yards to go to capture those cannons. And that was when all four big guns went off at the same time. BOOM!!!

A huge hole was blasted in the center of the first company. Two dozen men were literally knocked down by the enemy canister. Poor Sgt. Charlie Hill, the 2nd Regiment's standard bearer, had his right forearm blown clear off. With his left hand he gave the national flag to one of the color corporals, then he passed out.

The screams of the wounded and dying men were just horrible. One minute the attack was in full swing; the next minute everyone was trying to get back across the river to safety. That full battery volley was just devastating, stopping the attackers dead in their tracks.

"Run! Or we'll all be killed!" shouted several men from Company A as they dashed through Company B's ranks on their way to safety.

Joshua helped one of the wounded men limp back across the land bridge. He didn't know the fellow. He was probably one of the canister victims from Company A. The man had taken a hit in the thigh. His pants leg was a bloody mess, but with Joshua's help he was making it back to friendly territory.

While helping the wounded man back to safety Joshua glanced over his shoulder and saw five dead men on the far side of the bridge. The retreat was a ragged mess, with twenty or more wounded men being helped along by their comrades. When everyone got back to the rifle pits, the force was nothing but a mob. It took over ten minutes to reform the regiment.

After the 2nd Regiment reformed General Newton called for another officer's meeting.

"Gentlemen, I would like your opinions on why our attack failed," said General Newton.

Colonel Townsend looked at Major Lincoln, but it was Lt. Colonel Pearsall who spoke up first.

"Sir, perhaps we did not spend enough time softening up the enemy with our artillery before the infantry attack," said Pearsall.

Major Lincoln nodded in agreement. "I agree; we need to neutralize the enemy's artillery before we attack next time."

The general thought for a moment, then said, "Very well. I want our artillery to concentrate on knocking out the enemy cannons." He turned to his aid-de-camp, "Make it so."

The Union artillery opened up a steady fire at the enemy batteries. It wasn't long before the Confederate guns replied in kind. An artillery duel ensued.

"Joe, we need to keep our heads down," said Joshua.

Shells were arching over their position, landing some two hundred yards or more behind them. Then one shell hit right in the middle of a large oak tree that was standing about twenty yards behind Company B. The tree exploded with several limbs flying high into the air. The limbs cart wheeled through space. Joshua looked up to see one limb flying right towards him. He ducked as it crashed mere feet from him and Joe.

"Dang! Dat was close!" exclaimed Joe.

"Hey, it almost took your head off," joked Joshua.

"Dat ain't funny, Josh."

The artillery duel continued for a solid hour. General Newton watched it with his binoculars. He was disappointed in the results. It seemed like most of the shots were passing harmlessly over the rebel battery.

"Tell those gunners to depress their guns," ordered Newton.

The general watched shells slamming into the ground in front of the rebel battery. Dirt from the explosions rained down on the Kilcrease Artillery.

"Now we're cooking!" said the general.

Finally, a shell landed right beside one of the cannons. The explosion flipped the cannon over. The gun's wheel smashed to pieces on impact. The man standing closest to the explosion was thrown high into the air. One of the gun crew standing on the opposite side of the cannon was crushed when the gun landed on top of him, killing him instantly. And the rest of the gun crew was severely injured.

"Excellent!!! Colonel Townsend have your regiment prepare for another assault on the enemy," the general ordered. "And Colonel Pearsall, I want you to hold most of your regiment in reserve, but pick out your three best companies and have them support the attack from south of the land bridge. Oh, and have them dig rifle pits as close to the river as is practical."

The plan this time was for the left wing of the 2nd Regiment to advance in columns of fours until they reached the other side of the land bridge. At that time they would go into a line of battle and attack with all four companies. Meanwhile, the right wing would offer support by firing at the oblique from the banks of the river. South of the land bridge, a battalion of the 99th Colored Infantry would fire at rebel positions opposite them, lending support to Major Lincoln's men.

"All right, Company B, fall in on Corporal Bates," ordered Captain Tracy.

Private Joshua Jackson lined up next to the corporal. His buddy, Joe Henry, was just to his left, and tall Sam Clark was in the rear rank behind him. The company was short five men. One was killed when he was shot through the throat, and four were wounded in the full battery volley that broke the attack.

"I reckon we're lucky we weren't the lead company in that attack," Joshua told Joe.

"Yeah, Company A got clobbered," replied Joe.

"All right, quiet in the ranks!" shouted Sgt. Fisher.

General Newton, Colonel Townsend, Lt. Col. Pearsall and Major Lincoln walked to a central position in front of the formation. Once again Major Lincoln's troops would spearhead the attack. The general turned to Major Lincoln and commented, "Major, I have every confidence that your men will carry the enemy position."

Major Benjamin Lincoln looked over his troops. They

were good men and he was proud to be an officer in the U.S.C.T., however, getting over this land bridge was becoming quite a challenge. The Confederates had an easily defended position. In fact, it reminded him of the pass at Thermopylae where 300 Spartans held off the entire Persian army.

"Sir, you can count on my men to do their best," said Lincoln.

The general stood tall and addressed the troops.

"Men, in just a few minutes you will be attacking the Rebel position. Please remember why you are here. You are fighting to restore the Union! You are fighting to put an end to slavery! And you are fighting to bring honor to your regiment! Good luck and God bless the United States of America!"

The men cheered wildly, waving their caps in the air.

"General, you don't need to worry. We're Lincoln's boys and we'll get the job done!" shouted Joshua.

Joe slapped Joshua on the back, "You're damn right we will!"

"Attention, regiment!" shouted Colonel Townsend.

"Shoulder, arms!"

"Right, face!" Immediately the formation went from two ranks into a column of four ranks.

"Forward, march!"

As the column approached the natural bridge Colonel Townsend's battalion veered to the right, while Major Lincoln's battalion continued straight ahead.

Col. Townsend ordered his men into a line of battle and halted them at the edge of the river. He had them firing at the Confederates while Lincoln's battalion continued across the natural bridge. To the south of the natural bridge Lt. Col. Pearsall's men began firing at the Milton Artillery and First Florida Reserves.

Once on the other side of the bridge, Major Lincoln ordered his battalion into a line of battle. The men quickly moved into position.

"Battalion, ready!" shouted Lincoln.

"Aim!"

"Fire!"

Kaboom!

A giant cloud of smoke rolled towards the rebels.

"Forward, march!"

For the second time today, Joshua advanced into the Jaws of Death. Cannons roared at the Union battle line; muskets rattled. He heard bullets buzzing by his ears. The whole scene was a hellish inferno. Joshua just knew he was not going to live to see the sunset.

The world became a hectic, confusing swirl of light and sound. Joshua concentrated on following the captain's orders, shutting out all the distractions around him.

The order to fire by file was given. At the very instant Joshua and the man behind him, Sam, fired their muskets, Sam took a bullet right in the middle of his forehead. He collapsed like a sack of potatoes.

As they got closer to the enemy Joshua could see more and more of his company going down.

"Close it up!" shouted Sergeant Fisher. His men quickly

filled in the gaps left by the fallen.

Then, with just thirty-five yards to go, the cannon right in front of Company B fired canister. Right after the blast, the world went silent, except for the ringing in Joshua's ears. When the smoke cleared, he saw many of his comrades on the ground, dead or wounded. He looked to his right where he saw both Captain Tracy and Sgt. Fisher dead. But what he saw next totally shocked him. His best friend, Joe Henry, was mortally wounded.

Joshua kneeled down and cradled his friend's head in his arms. A tear ran down his cheek. "This ain't happenin'. It can't be."

"Is it bad, Josh?"

Joshua unbuckled Joe's belt and unbuttoned his sack coat. Joe's shirt was a crimson mess. He had taken a canister ball in the gut and was losing blood rapidly.

The look on Joshua's face told Joe just how bad it was.

"Josh, I never told you this, but when my ma passed away the only thing she left me was a brooch. I've been carrying it around in my haversack and I wancha to give it to Pearl. She lives at 415 Rue Dauphine, New Orleans. Please promise me you'll look her up and tell her I loved her."

"I promise, Joe. I swear I'll give it to her."

Joe coughed, and spittle of blood ran down his chin.

"Are ya still there, Josh? It's getting dark and I'm so cold."

And those were Joe Henry's last words. Joshua sobbed at the loss of his best friend.

The Union attack had failed again. Major Lincoln's battalion was falling back in retreat. Soldiers were passing Joshua as he continued to hold his friend's body. Then Joshua realized he needed to go with the rest of his company or he might be captured. He took off Joe's haversack and slung it over his shoulder. Grabbing his musket he rose and double timed it back across the natural bridge. It bothered him that he had to leave his friend's body just laying on the battle-field, but what choice did he have?

General Sherman said it best when he said, "War is Hell!" He was so right!

Chapter 11

"There they go again, Gene," Luther said.

Shells began arching over the Confederate breastworks. Once again, limbs of trees and bits of bark began to fly as a result. The Union artillerists were aiming too high but I kept my head down just in case.

It's funny how you feel when the enemy is shelling your position. It's just like the feeling you get when you are caught in the middle of a wide open field in a thunderstorm. At any second you could be hit by lighting and you can't do a thing about it. At least when infantry is attacking you feel you have some control; you can fight back. But when shells are dropping out of the sky, you're at the mercy of the Fates and you feel so terribly helpless.

Captain Johnson made his way down his company's line, checking on each and every boy. "I'm proud of the way ya'll have handled yourselves under fire," he told us.

"Thank you, sir. We're here to do our part!" Luther replied.

"Yes, son, duty first," agreed our captain.

I was listening to the conversation between Captain Johnson and Luther with one part of my mind, but mostly I was thinking back to the previous attack. It had started with enemy shelling, just like what was happening now. I was watching the Kilcrease Artillery firing their cannons, when all of a sudden a shell landed right next to one of their guns. The image of the explosion was still imprinted on my mind. I could see one man flying through the air and another being crushed by the big gun when it landed on him. It was just awful.

When the Yankees attacked it all happened so quickly. They came over the natural bridge in a column of fours, then deployed into a line of battle. Our captain gave the order to fire at will and we all began to fire our muskets at our own pace.

"Don't expose yourselves unnecessarily!" shouted Prof. Melton.

While one group of Yanks came at us from across the "bridge," the other group fired at us from the far side of the river, forcing us to keep our heads down as much as possible.

It was during this time that the most comical thing happened on that eventful day. There was a sweet gum tree standing about ten feet behind the breastworks and a little to my left. Behind the tree I saw our two youngest cadets, Frank Damon and Henry DeMilly, one behind the other, and they were both holding up a flintlock musket that was bigger than they were. Little Frankie pulled the trigger. Blam! The kick of the recoil knocked both boys completely off their feet, right onto their butts!!! It was just too funny!

Meanwhile, back at the field hospital, wounded soldiers were being carried back to the Byrd cabin where the surgeons were busy operating. Casualties were still relatively light after two major assaults by the enemy. In spite of that, it was never a pretty sight to see wounded men, with the pain and physical suffering that they must endure.

The two cadets that were assigned orderly duties, Tom Archer and John Milton, were busy helping move the patients, and when needed, to hold them down. They were also recruited to administer the chloroform to knock out the patients during the operations and to make sure they stayed out.

Just after the first assault, a private was brought in with a bullet in the upper right arm. The surgeon from Quincy decided that the arm would need to be amputated. He told Tom Archer to give the patient some chloroform. Tom poured a little chloroform on a rag and held it over the man's nose. The patient was out like a light.

The surgeon first cut through the muscle with his scalpel, and then he began to saw the bone. About half way through the bone, the man suddenly woke up.

"Ahiiiieeeeeee!!!!!!!!!" he screamed.

"Quick, give that man some more chloroform!" ordered

the doctor.

While John Milton held the man down, Tom poured more chloroform on the rag. In just a few seconds the man was back to sleep.

The rest of the operation went well. The man would live, but minus one arm.

Another interesting thing occurred at the Byrd cabin that day. Mrs. Byrd had told her two children, Nancy and Alex, to stay out of the way by sitting quietly on the front porch. What Nancy, the older of the two children, saw next would stay with her for the rest of her long life.

A soldier had been shot in the hand and the surgeon had to cut off three of the man's fingers. The surgeon walked out onto the porch and threw the three fingers into the yard. Some hogs came over and ate them up with relish. The sight of the hogs eating the man's fingers horrified the children.

Although the Union battalion got closer on the second attempt to breach our defenses, it failed as well. There was just too much fire power concentrated on that small piece of real estate. The Union soldiers were bravely attempting the impossible.

We had been up since dawn, marched from New Port to here, and then been a part of the defense of Natural Bridge. It was nearly mid-afternoon and I thought to myself that this was the longest day of my life. Every minute in battle felt like an hour. Then the enemy started firing their cannons at us again. That could only mean that another attack was coming.

The afternoon was beginning to warm up and I got a strong thirst. I tipped up my canteen to suck out the last drops of water.

"Luther, you got any water left in your canteen?"

"Sure, you want some?"

He handed me his canteen and I took a nice long pull on it. The water was so refreshing.

"Thanks pal," I said. "I owe you one."

"Yeah, maybe one day when you're Governor you will remember me," he said with a laugh.

The Union shelling seemed to be slowing down.

"Do you think they're getting low on ammunition?" I asked Luther.

"Heck, I hope they run out!" he replied.

I peeked over the breastwork, but still there was no sign of the expected infantry attack.

"Oh, by the way, I've been meaning to ask you what that kiss on the cheek was all about back at the train station?"

"Gosh, Gene, that was totally unexpected. I didn't even know Sue liked me. Besides, there's a girl back home by the name of Jerusia that I kind of fancy."

"Just how serious is that?"

"Well, after the war is over and I graduate from the seminary, I might decide to court her," he said thoughtfully.

After a few more minutes the shelling stopped. We knew what was coming next. The Yanks were coming again.

"Here they come, lads!" shouted Captain Johnson. "Now, do not fire until I give the order."

I peeked over the breastworks and saw what looked like a full regiment in column of fours coming right at us. They were giving this attack their all. But we were waiting for them.

They deployed into two lines of battle, one behind the other, and came at us at a fast pace. We still held our fire.

"Wait for it!" ordered our captain.

The Yankees halted and fired at us by battalion. When I saw them raise their muskets and aim at us, I ducked low, keeping my head down. I heard the enemy fire at us and saw one of Captain Houstoun's men literally spin around after being shot. Holding his shoulder he collapsed to the ground in agony.

I heard General Miller shout, "Prepare to fire by company from the right!"

"Fire!"

Colonel Daniels' seven companies on the far right opened up one after the other, working from right to left. The Milton Artillery fired its three cannons. Then Colonel Love's militia fired a volley, and the Kilcrease Artillery fired its three remaining cannons.

Now, it was our turn, and Captain Johnson hollered at the top of his voice, "Company, ready!"

"Aim!"

"Fire!"

Every cadet pulled his musket's trigger at the same time. KABLAM! A cloud of smoke rolled toward the attacking Union line. Immediately I began to reload my rifle. I poured the contents of a paper cartridge down my musket's barrel. I quickly rammed the charge to the bottom of the barrel. Then I put a percussion cap on the firing nipple of my Enfield, and was ready to shoot. While I was loading my musket, Colonel Girardeau's militia companies on the far left finished up the company firing.

We Confederate defenders had poured an enormous amount of lead into the attacking enemy. When the smoke cleared we could see the "Blue Bellies" heading back to the safety of the other side of the river. Once again we had beaten them back.

Every cadet gave the rebel yell at the sight of the Yanks retreating.

I was sure that this time we had beaten them for good. Apparently General Miller believed this to be the case as well. The good general gave us the order to fix bayonets and charge as the last Union soldiers were skedaddling.

With a yell of victory we hopped up and ran down the slope ahead of the militiamen. I saw well over a hundred Union casualties as I jogged toward the land bridge. One soldier in particular caught my attention. He was trying to get up, but seemed very unsteady, and I noticed he had blood running down the side of his head. It looked to me like he had received a bullet's glancing blow to the side of his skull.

I decided to make him my prisoner. However, just as I got to him Eddie Northrup ran up.

"Put your hands up!" I shouted at the wounded soldier who quickly complied.

"Don't take him prisoner, Eugene. Run the black bastard through!" Eddie shouted as he lowered his bayonet tipped rifle in preparation to deliver the lethal thrust.

I wasn't about to let Eddie kill this defenseless fellow who had just surrendered to me. With lightning speed I

125

knocked his musket away with my own musket, hitting his left fingers in the process.

"Ouch!!! What in the hell are you doing!" he shouted.

"This man has surrendered to me and I'm not going to let you kill him." I calmly told him. "He's mine. Now, get!"

Eddie knew I meant business and without saying another word he continued on down the slope.

The Yanks had given up and were pulling out as fast as they could, heading back to their ships. Our men pursued them for a couple of miles before giving up the chase.

I gave my prisoner a good looking over. He was about my height and build. His eyes were wide with fear, maybe because of his brush with death moments ago. Although he was the enemy, I pitied him.

He was still bleeding from his head wound so I took out my handkerchief and tied it around his head. After a minute the bleeding stopped.

"Can you walk?" I asked.

"I think so."

"Good, then let's go."

We started up the slope. He wobbled a bit as he walked. His legs acted like they were made out of rubber. Clearly, he was still shaky from his head wound. I felt sorry for the poor soul.

I asked him, "You got a name?"

"Private Joshua Jackson."

"Where are you from?"

"Virginia," he said as he put out his hand to steady himself on a pine tree.

"Sorry, sir, but I feel like I'm goin' to faint. I feel dizzy."

"Then take a seat," I told him and pointed at the base of the tree.

He sat down, leaning back against the pine. He closed his eyes and gave a little moan.

Looking back toward the natural bridge, I could see our troops returning from pursuing the enemy. Some were carrying their muskets on their shoulders, others carrying them in the "trail arms" position, and still others had their weapons slung. They slowly straggled in. Some of them were bringing prisoners back with them as well.

The men with prisoners saw me and my wounded Federal resting by the pine tree and decided that was as good a place to collect all of our prisoners of war as any other. After a few minutes General Miller and Captain Johnson walked over to the little knot of prisoners.

"Attention!" ordered a sergeant. We snapped to attention as the general walked up to us.

"At ease," General Miller said. "Men, I'm very proud of the way you fought today. I see we have captured about three dozen Federals. Good work!"

He turned to Captain Johnson and patted him on the back, "Your cadets were very brave today. You can be proud of them. Now, I want you to pick out some of your best boys to escort the prisoners to Tallahassee."

"Very good, sir," responded Johnson.

Captain Johnson picked eight of his best from the Cadet Corps to act as guards. They were Cadet Lt. Byrd Coles, Cadet Sgt. John DuBose, Charles Beard, Egbert Nims, William Quaile, Luther Tucker, John Winthrop, and I.

Our captain pulled Lt. Byrd Coles aside, "Lieutenant, I

want you to supervise this escort detail to Tallahassee. Have each of your seven cadet guards pick out five prisoners to be responsible for. March the prisoners to Woodville and ride the train into town. Once you get to town take them to the Masonic Hall."

"Sir, what about those prisoners that are badly wounded?" asked Coles.

"Ah, a good question," said Capt. Johnson. "How many severely wounded prisoners do we have?"

"I believe we have half a dozen that need immediate medical attention."

"Alright, if the prisoner is too wounded to walk to Woodville, then use that mule drawn wagon over there to take them up to the field hospital. I'm assigning Cadets John Winthrop and Egbert Nims to drive them up. When they get there they will relieve Cadets Tom Archer and John Milton. I want Archer and Milton to fall in with the rest of the cadets when we return to Tallahassee. Have Cadets Winthrop and Nims stay at the Byrd cabin until the wounded prisoners are well enough to travel."

"I'll see to it, sir," Lt. Coles said with a salute.

Chapter 12

We helped load the wounded men into the wagon. It was a tight fit but somehow we squeezed the six men into the back of it. John gave rein to the mule and off they went.

The rest of the prisoners were either slightly wounded or just too slow to escape the pursuing rebels and thus were captured. I picked out five prisoners to escort to town, one of whom was Joshua Jackson. Pvt. Jackson was feeling better and he could walk with a steady gait now.

"Are you well enough to walk a few miles?" I asked him.

"I reckon I can make it. I don't feel so dizzy any mo. But I still got a mighty big headache, like somebody hit me wid a hammer."

We watched the rest of the Cadet Corps start marching

toward Woodville. They marched with a spring in their step, victors of a great battle! The fife player began playing Dixie and several of the boys gave a cheer.

Lt. Byrd Coles got us started down the dirt road toward Woodville. We had our bayonets attached to our loaded muskets, hopefully we would not need to use our weapons, but you just never knew when a prisoner might try to escape.

The afternoon was waning as we escorted our prisoners down the wagon trail. Luther came over to me and said in a low voice, "You'll never believe what I saw while we were pursuing the Yanks."

"What was it?"

"Well, we chased the Yanks for over a mile down the river before giving up. On the way back I was searching along the river bank for any wounded when I saw him."

"You saw who?" I asked.

"I saw a colored soldier laying at the edge of the river, and he was barely alive."

"So?"

"There's more. I saw a log floating down the river. Or rather, I though it was a log. But no, it moved toward the wounded man, and the next thing I knew a huge pair of jaws latched on to the man's arm and dragged him into the water with the man screaming for help. It was dreadful! In just seconds there was no sign of the man, except some bubbles on the surface of the water where he was last seen before the creature pulled him down into the dark depths."

"Dang, a gator got him," I said.

"Yep."

The wagon trail to Woodville was fairly straight, so for quite a distance we could see the Cadet Corps ahead of us. But, as time went by, they gradually pulled further and further ahead of us, until about half way there, we could no longer see them.

By the time we got to Woodville, it was getting dark. I thought for sure the last train to Tallahassee would have already left the station, but no, Captain Johnson had ordered the engineer to wait for us. Thank God. If we hadn't caught this train we would have had to find a secure building to house all our prisoners for the night and I doubt that Lt. Byrd Coles was that familiar with this small town.

Our captain had reserved a freight car for the prisoners. Once the prisoners were inside the freight car, we slid the door closed and locked it. Our guard detail joined the rest of the cadets, and once everyone was onboard the train, we began traveling north.

Beside the cadets, there were many other veterans of the battle on the train. And the body of the only Tallahasseean to be killed in the battle was onboard, Captain Henry Simmons.

As we approached Bel Air we could hear a crowd of people clapping and cheering for us. Several local families had traveled down to the resort to be closer to the action; it was only nine miles from the battlefield, as the crow flies. Many of the girls from the seminary took the train down to join their families and be among the first to greet the conquering heroes.

The train slowed as it pulled into the Bel Air station. I could hear the girls singing Dixie, but with these words:

The young cadets were the first to go
To meet and drive away the foe
Look away! Look away! Look away!
Dixie Land.

The moment the train stopped several girls jumped on board and placed an olive wreath on the brow of each cadet. Sue Archer found her brother, Tom, and placed a wreath on his head. Then she saw Luther and gave him such a hug. She placed a wreath on his head and whispered something into his ear. He blushed red.

Then she looked up to me with her big brown eyes, and placed the conqueror's wreath upon my brow.

"Eugene, we are so proud of you and all the cadets that fought in the great battle to save Tallahassee from the Invader."

"Gee, thanks," was all I could manage.

A big brass band was playing on the platform when the train pulled into Tallahassee. The crowd at the train station was enormous in spite of the late hour. It looked like the entire town had come to the station to welcome home their heroes, and everyone was curious to find out what had happened in the battle that day.

Governor John Milton was there to greet us. He came

over to where we were exiting the train and shook each cadet's hand as we disembarked.

The governor gave me a firm hand shake as I stepped onto the platform. He was clean shaven with graying hair and a rather large nose.

"God bless you for what you did today. I'm very proud of you," he told each of us.

As we made our way through the crowd many gentlemen slapped us on the backs and congratulated us for our victory. It was all so overwhelming.

But my biggest surprise of the evening was when I saw Ma and Pa on the platform. Pa must have driven the carriage over from Monticello. I was so happy to see them, especially my Ma, whom I hadn't seen since the Christmas break and I must admit I really missed her.

Ma gave me a bear hug. If she had hugged me any harder I believe I would have popped like a squeezed pimple!

I asked her, "When did you find out about the Yankees landing at St. Marks?"

"Well, Reverend Brooks informed us before he started his sermon on Sunday. It caused quite a stir you can imagine. In fact, a couple of men got up and rushed out of the church to get their guns." She continued, "We drove the carriage over to Tallahassee on Sunday afternoon, and have been waiting for your return ever since."

"Did you hear any of the battle?" I asked.

"Oh, yes! From this morning until mid-afternoon we could hear cannon fire coming from south of town," said my Pa. "It sounded like one heck of a fight! And your dear Ma was so worried about you."

"Shucks! I was fine. I didn't even get a scratch," I bragged.

"Well, we didn't know that," said Ma. "Thank God you're safe."

"Yes, ma'am," I replied.

Cadet Lieutenant Byrd Coles tapped me on the shoulder. "I'm sorry to interrupt, but we need to march our prisoners to the Masonic Hall."

A moment later Lt. Coles shouted, "Guard Detail, fall in!"

The eight of us in the guard detail quickly formed up and marched the short distance to the freight car with the prisoners. Cadet Sergeant DuBose unlocked the car's door, slid it back, and out stumbled about thirty Union soldiers. We proceeded to march them down Gaines Street, and then up Duval Street to the Masonic Hall where they would be kept under guard until they could be sent to Andersonville, Georgia.

When we got to the Masonic Hall I turned to Pvt. Jackson and said, "Good luck. I hope you survive the war."

"Thanks." And then in a low voice he said, "And thanks for saving ma life."

After locking up the prisoners, seven of us marched back to the dormitory. We left Cadet Charles Beard as the prisoners' first guard of the evening, and when Cadet Lt. Coles got back to campus he would make up a roster of guards for the next twenty-four hours.

By the time I got back to my dorm room, I was completely beat. I felt like I had marched from Tallahassee to Timbuktu. There was a painful blister on my big right toe that was hurting like the dickens. I hadn't mentioned it to my Ma because I didn't want her to worry about me.

Luther jumped into the top bunk with his uniform still on, and within two minutes he was snoring away. I decided he had the right idea and following his example, fell into bed with everything on except my boots.

What a day.

Chapter 13

he very next day a funeral with full military honors was planned for Captain Henry Simmons. It would be held at his church, St. John's Episcopal. An honor guard of cadets was requested to participate and Captain Johnson picked me to be in that detail. Cadet Sgt. John DuBose would lead the detail with the honor of carrying the flag during the funeral procession.

The church was packed full of people paying their final respects. Many friends of the Simmons family and all of the captain's cavalry company were in attendance.

We sat up front, on the left side of the church. In the center front pew sat the widowed wife. The widow was dressed in black from head to toe. She wore a black dress with black crape trim on her collar and cuffs, and a widow's veil covered her face. On the far right of the front pew sat several officers from the 5th Florida Cavalry Regiment, including its commander, Colonel Scott.

At the front of the church I saw the coffin with a Confederate flag draped over it, and at the coffin's head burned the paschal candle. I hadn't ever seen a flag draped over a coffin before, but I thought it was a good idea. It gave the departed soldier's coffin a certain dignity, a symbol of the cause for which he died.

Colonel Scott walked up to the coffin. After a moment he turned to address everyone. He told us how brave, courageous, and loyal a soldier Captain Simmons had been. He said there had been no finer officer serving his country than the good captain, and everyone in the 5th Florida Cavalry would miss him immensely.

With that comment, the widow began to sob uncontrollably. Of course, no one would miss him as much as his own dear wife and infant. I felt so sorry for her. And to make things worse, rumor had it that the poor man was killed on his birthday! How tragic is that?

After the priest gave his eulogy, we all filed out of the church. Six strong troopers from the captain's cavalry company served as pall bearers. They carried the coffin out the church door and slid it onto a waiting hearse pulled by two black horses with tall black plumes.

As the funeral procession started down Call Street I heard the church bell begin to toll. Colonel Scott, on horseback, led the procession down the street. Next, our cadet color guard followed close behind the colonel. The flag that Sgt. DuBose carried was cased in canvas, as was the tradition at a funeral, and it had two black streamers attached to the flag staff, symbols of mourning.

Right behind our color guard I could hear the clip clop of the two black horses pulling the hearse. Behind the hearse came a rider-less horse. It was Captain Simmons' trusty steed. A sergeant from the 5th Florida Cavalry walked beside the animal, holding the reins.

Behind the captain's horse walked his widowed wife and the rest of his family, followed by the captain's company of men, slow marching to the muffled beat of a single drummer. Bringing up the rear were all the friends of the family, and there were many.

The procession walked west on Call Street until it reached the city cemetery. Near the middle of the cemetery was an open grave. In a short time a large crowd of people had gathered around it to see the captain put to rest.

After lifting the coffin off of the hearse, the pall bearers folded up the flag, then lowered the coffin into the grave. Colonel Scott gave the flag to the widow as a keepsake.

Cadet Sergeant DuBose called our honor guard to attention.

"Load!"

I quickly pulled a cartridge out of my cartridge box, bit off the end of the paper cartridge and poured the powder and bullet down my barrel. Then I rammed it all home, and placed a percussion cap on my weapon.

"Ready!"

"Aim!"

"Fire!"

BOOM!!!

We did this two more times as a final salute to a fine officer who had made the ultimate sacrifice for his country.

The priest offered a final prayer for the soul of the dearly departed. When he finished, the sobbing widow threw herself on her husband's grave, weeping in such a manner that it brought a tear to my eye.

Chapter 14

*T*he rest of the week following the battle went by in a blur. The town was in such excitement over the victory. If any of us went off campus, the town's people would congratulate us and make a big fuss over us. It was embarrassing, yet it made me feel important. All I could think about all week was what I would tell Jenny when I saw her again. When I wasn't busy with drill and such, I was daydreaming about looking into her azure eyes. I longed to see her sweet smile again.

Sunday morning rolled around and I was up at the crack of dawn. I was hoping that Jenny had returned from Thomasville and would be at the Presbyterian Church for this morning's service. I shaved myself with my straight razor, shined my boots, put on my uniform, and combed my hair.

"Luther, are you ready to go to church yet?" I asked.

"What's the big hurry? The church is still going to be there next week!" Luther chuckled.

"Very funny, you know why I'm in such a rush to get to church."

"Oh, hang on to your horses. All I need to do is put on my boots and I'm ready to go."

We walked up Clinton Street. My blister was healing well and I found the climb up the hill was not too painful to my toe. Turning left onto Adams we could see the white spire of the Presbyterian Church just up ahead.

As we approached the church I asked Luther about his plans.

"Would you like to come to the Presbyterian Church with me today?"

"No thanks, Gene, I appreciate the offer, but I have lots of news to tell my friends at the Methodist Church. I'll see you later back at the dorm."

We parted with a hand shake, and I climbed the steps to greet a couple of the church's deacons. They were both dressed in gray frock coats and were wearing top hats. They gave me a warm welcome as I entered the sanctuary.

I looked down the left aisle and saw the MacLaren family sitting in the same pew as before. And there was Jenny. She was wearing a pink and cranberry plaid dress, and her bonnet was the color of raspberries.

I sat down in the pew behind them, and when Jenny saw me her face lit up. She leaned closer to her father and whispered, "Papa, may we invite Gene to sit with us?"

Mr. MacLaren looked back at me and I saw a look of

approval on his face. Then he turned to his daughter and said, "Yes, my dear, we would be honored to have him sit with us."

With a twinkle in her eye she said, "There's room up here for one more."

"It would be my pleasure to sit with you all," I replied.

The MacLaren family shifted to the left to open up a spot next to the aisle for me. As I sat down next to Jenny, she gave me a sweet smile. I could tell she was delighted to have me sitting next to her. What an angel sent from heaven above, I thought to myself.

The choir began the worship service with the hymn "A Mighty Fortress is Our God". With the church organ backing them, the choir sang it with such power and majesty that goose bumps went up and down my spine.

Before Rev. DuBose began his sermon he made the following announcement. "Last Monday a battle was fought south of town to prevent the Yankees from capturing the state capital. Cadets from our own seminary took part in this defense, and I am happy to see one of their numbers sitting in the congregation this morning. Young man, would you please stand for a moment?"

Oh, my! How embarrassing. I stood up and everyone in the church turned to look at me. Then to my surprise they began to clap, and that was something I had never heard in church before. I made a slight bow to acknowledge their applause.

"Our church wishes to honor those cadets who took part in the Battle of Natural Bridge, so this coming Saturday night we are having a special dinner in our fellowship hall in their honor. I sincerely hope the Cadet Corps will be able to attend," said the pastor.

When I took my seat again Jenny whispered into my ear, "You will come next Saturday, won't you?"

I whispered back, "I wouldn't miss it for the world."

The pastor's sermon was about David and the Philistine giant, Goliath. He compared young David to our Confederate army, and of course, the Union army with the giant Goliath. It was an interesting lesson and I enjoyed it all the more because Jenny was sitting next to me.

After the worship service was over I went outside and everyone wanted to shake my hand and congratulate me. They were making such a fuss over me that I was sure I would end up with a very big head. Mr. MacLaren was especially proud of me and said brave young men like me might yet save the South.

"Thank you, sir, but I was just doing my duty. By the way, how is your bookstore doing?" I asked.

"Well, I'm selling just enough books to stay in business. It's tough these days because the Confederate dollar is getting weaker and weaker, which means I'm constantly putting up my book prices due to inflation. And with inflation so high these days I'm losing customers."

"I'm sorry to hear that. Maybe when the war is over business will pick up again."

"Hopefully, it will," he replied.

Jenny took her father by the arm and with the look of a pitiful puppy inquired, "Papa, could we have Gene over for lunch today, please."

But before her parents could reply I declined the offer.

"I would love to have lunch with ya'll once again, but unfortunately I have guard duty from one o'clock until three o'clock this afternoon."

"Oh, fiddlesticks, on the military!" Jenny pretended to pout.

"I'm sorry, but duty calls. I'll see you again at church on Saturday night."

We said our farewells and I rushed off to get ready for guard duty at the Masonic Hall.

Cadet Sergeant John McCall, nicknamed "Ole Blue Eyes", marched me over to the Masonic Hall. I relieved Billy Perkins, who I'm sure was happy to see me marching up to take over as guard.

Since the Battle of Olustee, some thirteen months ago, the Masonic Hall had been used as a prison for wounded enemy soldiers. When the Free Masons built their hall they built a solid building with small windows that often had its heavy curtains drawn. The Masons usually kept their curtains closed because they were a secret society and didn't want the general population knowing what went on during their secret meetings.

In February 1864 a major battle was fought just east of Lake City at a place known as Olustee. Wounded Union soldiers were brought to Tallahassee by rail and a secure place was needed to house them. That was when the Mayor of Tallahassee asked the Masonic Grand Master if those wounded men could be kept at their hall until they were well enough to make the long trip to Andersonville Prison. The Grand Master approved and the very next day the Masons installed iron bars in the windows to prevent any prisoners from escaping.

From that time on, the Masonic Hall, located at the west corner of Duval and McCarthy Streets, was used by the city as a prison for wounded enemy soldiers. As those Union prisoners became strong enough to undertake the journey they were escorted north to Andersonville.

I was instructed to patrol the front of the building. The only way in and out of the hall was through the front door which was kept locked. I had the key and the only time I was allowed to open the door was when a doctor or nurse came to check on the patients.

As I walked to and fro with fixed bayonet I wondered how the Union private I had captured was doing. His head wound didn't look that serious to me, but you never can tell about wounds. Captain Johnson told us about a man in his old regiment that had simply scraped his knee on a rock during a skirmish with the Yanks. It became infected, and a week later he was dead. You just never knew if a wound would heal or lead to your demise.

Now what did that fellow say his name was? I think he said it was Joshua Jackson. Yes, that's it.

As I passed a window I called out, "Private Jackson." No response. On the way back I called out again, "Private Jackson."

"Whatcha want, reb?"

"I was just wondering how you were doing," I said.

"My head is healin', but I got a big complaint."

"What's the matter?" I asked.

"Well, yesterday dat rebel dat nearly killed me while I be surrenderin' was on guard duty and he came in here and stole some of our stuff. He took a broach off of me dat belonged to my best friend. I was goin' to give it to my friend's lady friend in New Orleans someday, but I guess dat ain't happenin'."

I needed more information about this theft. It just was not right to steal from prisoners, although I had heard of this sort of thing happening before, yet as cadets we were expected to follow a high order of honor. I needed to report this to Captain Johnson when I returned to the seminary.

"When did this happen?" I asked.

"I ain't real sure. Um, it was startin' to get dark when he came in and took our stuff."

"What all was stolen?"

"Besides dat broach, he took a pocket watch off Corporal Williams, and a hand carved pipe off Private Brown."

"Alright, when I get back to the seminary I'll go straight to Captain Johnson and tell him about this injustice."

"Thanks, you're a good man," said Joshua.

I continued walking my post.

Gosh, that Eddie is one bad egg! He is not only a bully, but a thief as well. This injustice must not go unpunished!

Upon my return to the seminary I immediately proceeded to the principle's house and informed him of the crime. Captain Johnson could turn a blind eye to the whole affair, but I believed in his integrity, and I believed he would do something about this travesty of justice.

I knocked on the door and his wife opened it, "Can I help you?" she asked.

"Yes, ma'am, I need to see Captain Johnson."

"He is in the library studying. Please, come in."

His wife showed me into a room with shelves full of old books. Over by the window was a desk, and the captain was sitting at it reading a large book when I entered the room.

"Ah, Cadet Murray, what can I do for you?"

"Well, sir, while I was on guard duty this afternoon, one of the prisoners told me that he had a broach stolen from him by one of our cadet guards."

"I see. Do you have any idea who was the culprit?" Johnson asked.

"Yes, sir, the prisoner said it was the cadet who tried to kill him when he surrendered down at Natural Bridge. That would be Eddie Northrup. I know this because I'm the one who stopped Eddie from bayoneting the man."

"So, you think Edward Northrup was the thief?"

"Yes, sir."

"Well, I'm not surprised. Cadet Northrup has more demerits than anyone else at the military institute. Besides the broach, was there anything else stolen?"

"Yes, sir, a pocket watch, and a wood-carved pipe were also stolen."

"We will need to search his dorm room for these items," explained Johnson. "If we find the evidence I will have him expelled from the school."

"Follow me," said Captain Johnson.

We walked over to the dormitory, and after a thorough search, found the three items in a small cloth bag hid inside Eddie's canvas dirty clothes bag. The captain placed the stolen items on Eddie's bunk and moments later the thief walked in. I saw fear in his eyes as he took in what was going on in his dorm room.

"Cadet Northrup, where did you get these items?" Johnson asked.

"They're the spoils of war, sir," said Eddie with a smirk.

"You can wipe that smile off of your face, young man," ordered the captain. "Around here, theft is a serious crime, even theft from prisoners of war. I will not condone any form of theft, whether it is from a classmate or a prisoner of war, it's still stealing!"

"But, sir, they're just darkies," pleaded Northrup.

"Yes, they're Negroes and if they were slaves, they are ungrateful traitors, but theft of property, even of traitors, brings dishonor on this institution and on the thief. I will call for a Court Martial to be held at the earliest possible date."

"Sir, what am I to do until the trial?" asked Eddie.

"Mr. Northrup, you are hereby confined to your quarters until said Court Martial has come to a verdict," said Captain Johnson.

I knew how badly Private Jackson wanted his broach back so I asked our Principle if I could return the stolen items to their proper owners.

The captain thought for a moment.

"I'm sorry Cadet Murray, but we will need the items for the trial. They are considered evidence," Johnson explained. "After the Court Martial is over, then the items will be returned."

Later that afternoon I walked over to the Masonic Hall. Charlie was on guard duty and allowed me to go inside to talk with Private Jackson.

I explained everything that had taken place concerning the theft, and that he would have to be patient because the broach was needed in Eddie's trial.

"I understand, and I appreciate whatcha done," said Jackson.

When I got back to the dorm room I told Luther all about the upcoming Court Martial of Eddie. It was likely that the Court Martial Board would be made up of two or three professors, and I would assume Captain Johnson would be the chairman.

At colors the next morning Captain Johnson informed us of the date for the Court Martial. It was set for a week from today. The captain assigned Cadet Lt. Randolph to help defend Northrup.

Captain Johnson went down to the Masonic Hall and talked to Pvt. Jackson, Pvt. Brown, and Cpl. Williams. He told them that all three would need to appear before the Court Martial Board, give statements as to what happened on the day their items where stolen, and identify the thief.

The upcoming trial was the hot item of gossip all week. But with the stolen items found in Eddie's laundry bag, it was bound to be an open and shut case.

On Thursday night several of us cadets were sitting around chatting about the upcoming trial. What I found was that not all of us shared the same opinion about the matter.

"I don't know what all the fuss is about," said Patrick. "So what if Eddie took a few things from those darkies? They're our prisoners and we can do anything we want with them. Right?"

"Pat, I'm surprised that you would take Eddie's side in this," I commented. "And, no, we can't do anything we want

with our prisoners of war. If we want our Southern prisoners to be treated reasonably well, we need to treat the Yankee prisoners with a measure of respect. Besides, stealing is
stealing, and that's that."

Patrick scratched his chin in a thoughtful manner and
said, "I guess you've got a point there." Then he added, "I
just hate to see one of us expelled from the military institute."

A couple of the cadets agreed with Patrick. They didn't
like the idea of one of us being expelled, yet I felt that Eddie
deserved to be kicked out of the institute. I believed that
he lacked moral character and would only bring disgrace to
himself and the West Florida Seminary.

Chapter 15

At colors on Saturday morning Captain Johnson reminded us that the Presbyterian Church had invited the cadets who were veterans of the Battle of Natural Bridge to a banquet in their honor at six o'clock that evening. He encouraged everyone who was at the battle to attend the banquet.

"Cadets, please raise your hand if you plan on going tonight," the captain said.

About two dozen hands went up. And of course I stuck my hand high into the air, as I thought about the pleasure of Jenny's company at the banquet. In my mind's eye I could see her sweet smile and the way she looked at me with those big blue eyes. If there was anyway I could speed up the hands of the clock so that I could see her sooner, I would certainly do it right now.

Back in the dorm room Luther and I talked about the coming banquet. We looked forward to a big meal and some well deserved praise.

"I hear the Presbyterians are going to put on quite a spread of food for us tonight. I can hardly wait," commented Luther.

"Yeah, you're always hungry," I joked.

"My pa always said there were few pleasures in life better than a delicious meal prepared by a good cook," Luther said.

"Maybe some people appreciate food more than others do," I said with a chuckle.

"That could be."

"Anyway, what I'm looking forward to is seeing Jenny again," I said as I gave my boots a good brushing.

"She must be a really special girl," Luther speculated.

"You'll see. I'll introduce her to you this evening."

We marched from the campus with Captain Johnson in command. We looked sharp with our best uniforms on and our boots polished to a high shine. The captain halted us in front of the church.

"Break ranks, March!" commanded Johnson.

We fell out of formation, and I looked around to see if I could find Jenny, but there was no sign of her in front of the church.

We followed Captain Johnson into the fellowship hall. I looked around and spotted Jenny sitting with her mother and father on the far side of the room. The moment our eyes meet, Jenny's eyes lit up like Roman candles. I could tell she was overjoyed to see me.

"There she is," I told Luther, nodding in her direction. "Follow me."

We walked over to the table.

"Mr. and Mrs. MacLaren I would like to introduce you to my friend, Luther Tucker."

Mr. MacLaren stood up and shook Luther's hand, and then shook mine.

"And, Luther, this is Miss Jenny MacLaren."

Jenny gave us a pleasant smile, pointed to the chairs next to her, and asked, "Won't you please have a seat?"

I took the chair on Jenny's right and Luther sat down in the one on Jenny's left. We were sitting directly across from Jenny's parents who looked pleased to see me. A good sign, I thought to myself.

I looked around the hall. I spotted the Archer family with both Tom and his sister, Susan, sitting two tables over. Susan kept looking over at Luther.

I asked Jenny, in a voice I thought was low enough not to be heard by the others, "You're a friend of Sue Archer. Do you know if she fancies Luther?"

Jenny giggled. "Well, he is very handsome,"she explained.

"Yes, he is popular with the ladies," I commented.

"Excuse me, but I'm sitting right next to you two," said Luther with a rather red face.

"Oh, gracious me, pardon my manners!" exclaimed Jenny.

Mr. MacLaren leaned forward and cleared his throat. "Eugene, we were all very concerned about your safety when we heard about the cadets leaving to fight the Yankees."

"Yes, you could have been killed," said Jenny. "But I prayed that the angels would watch over you and keep you safe."

"Thanks," was all I said to that.

"Our professors made us keep our heads down during most of the fight," said Luther. "Still, with so much lead flying around, it's a miracle that none of us cadets was killed."

"Thank goodness ya'll made it through safely," said Mrs. MacLaren.

At the front of the room were a couple of long tables covered with all sorts of delicious food, the smell of which made my mouth water. To put together a meal like this during these hard times was a rarity and at the thought of such a scrumptious dinner my stomach began to rumble with hunger pains. I hoped Jenny wouldn't hear the noise my tummy was making. I'm really good it finding ways to embarrass myself you know!

Reverend John DuBose got up. He took his spoon and clanked it against his water glass to get the crowd's attention. Everyone in the hall quit talking.

"We are gathered together here to honor the cadets from the West Florida Seminary, who with courage and bravery, went out to meet the foe and, by the Good Lord's Providence, not only successfully defended our capital city, but came through the ordeal without loss of life. Surely, that was a miracle!"

The pastor continued, "Would every cadet that participated in the battle please stand."

The cadet veterans of the battle all stood as straight as ramrods, with their chests out. We were all full of pride! Everyone in the fellowship hall began to clap. I looked down at Jenny and saw her gazing up at me with a look of admiration.

After we sat back down the pastor gave a long prayer, asking for blessings on each and every cadet, our government leaders, our troops in the field, and finally on the food we were about to eat. As guests of honor we were allowed to get in line first to get our food. I piled my plate full of ham, roast chicken with corn bread dressing, black eyed peas, mashed potatoes, biscuits and gravy. And for dessert there was a delicious pear crisp and honey sponge cake. My, oh, my, eating this victory feast made me feel like a king!

"After a big meal like that, all I want to do is take a nap," I joked.

"Yes, a little soft music right now and I would be sleeping like a baby," Mr. MacLaren said with a chuckle.

Upon finishing our meal, we were entertained by the Campbell family with a medley of Scottish songs. Mr. Campbell played the guitar, his lovely wife was on the mandolin, and their two daughters sang and provided rhythm on the Celtic drum. They made some beautiful music and I really enjoyed it.

They say all good things must come to an end, and this evening of good food, good entertainment, and good company was coming to a close. I wish I had the power to stretch this wonderful moment in time and keep it going on forever, but alas, I am just a powerless mortal.

When the MacLaren family rose to leave I asked Jenny if I could escort her home.

"Of course, Gene, I would love to have you walk me home," she said as she lightly touched my arm.

It was a clear night with a half moon and a thousand stars, with little traffic on the street, just an occasional buggy passing by. Mr. and Mrs. MacLaren walked on ahead of us. Jenny and I walked hand in hand down the street.

"I'm glad your aunt in Thomasville has recovered from her illness. The whole time you were gone I couldn't think about anything but you," I told Jenny.

"And, you were constantly on my mind as well, Gene."

That was wonderful. She missed me as much as I had missed her.

We walked the two blocks to her house, enjoying each other's company, talking and laughing along the way. What a marvelous young lady she was. I was captivated by her smile and her big blue eyes made me weak in the knees. Was I falling in love?

Without stopping, her parents went inside the house, but as we approached the door, I slowed us down and we stopped on the front porch. We turned to face each other. I took both of her hands in mine and I gazed into her beautiful blue eyes.

"Jenny, I want to thank you and your church for a wonderful night," I said.

"We're all so very proud of you, Gene. You are more than welcome."

We stared into each others eyes for a moment. I gathered up some courage and whispered, "May I give you a good night kiss?"

She nodded.

We closed our eyes and this young cadet gave her a little kiss on the lips. I heard the angels sing. It was a perfect ending to a perfect night.

Historical Notes

Because of the Confederate victory at the Battle of Natural Bridge, Tallahassee was the only Confederate state capital east of the Mississippi River not captured by the Union. With General Johnston's surrender to General Sherman in North Carolina on 26 April 1865, the American Civil War came to an end. Federal forces under General McCook would not enter Tallahassee until May 10th. On that day, General Samuel Jones surrendered all Florida troops.

The story of the drummer boy falling off of the train is found only in the diary of Susan Archer. Since she is the only one to report this incident, there is some doubt whether it actually happened.

Cadet Luther Tucker was just 16 years old when he fought at Natural Bridge. On 4 April 1866 he married Jerusia Vause in Wakulla County. He is buried ten miles outside of Sopchoppy, Florida.

The author is a descendent of the family that allowed their cabin to be used as a field hospital during the battle. Alexander Byrd is his great-great-grandfather.

Captain Henry T. Simmons of Colonel Scott's 5th Florida Cavalry was the only soldier from Tallahassee to die in the battle. He was killed on his 36th birthday, leaving a grieving wife and infant behind.

From 10 May until early September 1865 Union troops used the West Florida Seminary dormitories for their barracks. That September the school opened its doors again, enrolling 58 male and 27 female students. The school would retain the name of the West Florida Seminary until 1901 when it became the Florida State College. In 1947 it became the Florida State University.

The Florida State University R.O.T.C. is one of only three colleges in the U.S. that have the honor of a battle streamer attached to their flag. The other two colleges are the Virginia Military Institute and the Citadel.

In several places in the story I refer to McCarty Street. This street is now known as Park Avenue.